RAVISHED BY THE MAN OF THE HOUSE

TEN BRATS WHO LEARN HOW TO PLEASE HIM

THRUST   KIMMY WELSH   WILLSIN ROWE
ZOE MORRISON   ABIGAIL BLACK   LENORE LOVE
KARLY DALTON   ELIZA DEGAULLE
CORDOVA SKYE   CANDY QUINN

SHAMELESS BOOK PRESS

This eBook is licensed for your personal enjoyment only. This eBook may not be re-sold or given away to other people. If you would like to share this book with another person, please purchase an additional copy for each recipient. If you're reading this book and did not purchase it, or it was not purchased for your use only, then please purchase your own copy. Thank you for respecting the hard work of this author.

Copyright 2017 Shameless Book Press

DISCLAIMER

All characters and events are entirely fictional and any resemblances to persons living or dead and circumstances are purely coincidental. All sex acts depicted occur between characters 18 years or older.

CONTENTS

About Shameless Book Deals   v

1. Doing Daddy - Thrust   1
2. A Night Full of Sin - Kimmy Welsh   19
3. Not a Little Girl Anymore - Abigail Black   37
4. My Daughter, My Wife, My New Life - Zoe Morrison   53
5. Pumpkin - Willsin Rowe   69
6. Ravishing Rhonda - Lenore Love   92
7. Step Inside my Heart - Karly Dalton   118
8. The Teacher's New Brat - Eliza DeGaulle   133
9. After Hours - Cordova Skye   157
10. First Time for the Man of the House - Candy Quinn   174

Shameless Book Deals   189
More from Shameless Book Press   190

ABOUT SHAMELESS BOOK DEALS

Get Free Erotica Downloads at Shameless Book Deals

Shameless Book Deals is a website that shamelessly brings you the very best erotica at the best prices from the best authors. Sign up to our newsletter to receive the following benefits from an erotica recommendation service with a difference:

Highly Specific Recommendations: Our system has been put together from the ground up so as to not lump all erotica under a single umbrella. While the service is gathering speed, a combined recommendation service is necessary, but as time goes on, our recommendations will get more specific based on erotica sub-genres, or kinks if you prefer. You choose the erotica sub-genres you want. We are the first to do this on such a scale.

Discreet: Although we are shameless we are also discreet. Our emails go straight to your inbox and our email subject lines will not be overly crass or vulgar. Graphics in our emails will be almost entirely book covers, more closely vetted than the eBook retailers are able to achieve. That said, the emails will be filled with erotica recommendations, so don't gather your friends and family around the computer when you read them if you don't want everybody to know what blows your hair back.

Professional: Shameless Book Deals is run by Scarlett Skyes, a #1 erotica author with an eye for quality erotica.

Quality: All authors/publishers are expected to hold to a high standard for their work and the deals they are offering to our subscribers. Check the Newsletter Submission Guidelines and report any authors that you believe have breached these guidelines. We recognize that not all complaints will be valid, but authors/publishers who are repeat offenders will be blacklisted to maintain the quality of our service.

Free Stories: Every subscriber gets access to a selection of FREE, and in some cases exclusive, erotica. Downloadable directly from our website.

DOING DADDY - THRUST

My little girl.

I've seen the way Lottie looks at me, the way she pretends she isn't. I know exactly what she wants, and tonight I've got the perfect excuse to give it to her.
So what if it's supposed to be wrong, or taboo, or exactly the opposite of what we should be doing, this girl is so hot she should come with a government warning, and I can't ignore it any more.
Lottie's going to get it hard, deep and unprotected, and then she's going to come back to me begging for more.

~

She's giving me that pouty, puppy dog look again that makes my dick so hard I think I'm going to faint. I've spent years fantasizing about *the* perfect girl, and she turns up here, after all this time, in exactly the place I shouldn't be looking for her.

She's so sexy she should be illegal, so horny she reduces

me to a mess of bare carnal desire and animalistic depravity - and that's me describing it lightly. Lottie, my eighteen-year-old step-daughter with those perfect perky, porn-star tits you could hang coats off, an ass like a ripened peach, fat juicy lips that tell me all I need to know about the shape of her pussy and a look in her eye that spells trouble in fat skyscraper-high letters.

She should come with a government health warning, she's that dangerous: a tear-out label that says *stay away, this girl is bad for your health*. If she's not walking around the house in tight fitting tops and tiny little skirts that barely cover her panties, she's giving me that look that says, *I know you want me, Daddy, and that makes my pussy wet, but it's too bad because little girls aren't meant to fuck their step-daddys, no matter how much it turns them on.*

The things I want to do to her would make the whole adult entertainment industry blush.

She's the typical teenage brat who likes to be in control, and it doesn't take a genius to work out that the way she flirts with me is a barely concealed attempt to become center of attention in a competition against her mom for my affection. The thing is, I don't think she realizes what the real consequences are going to be for playing so recklessly with a fire that can easily get out of control if left unguarded.

I don't know if deep down she really wants to fuck me, or whether she just gets off on teasing me with what she thinks I'll never be able to get from her, but it doesn't matter anyway, because now that we're finally alone, and I've got the perfect excuse to get the ball rolling, it's time to find out the truth, regardless of the consequences.

If Lottie gets all freaked out and refuses to come along for the ride, I'll tell her I was fooling around all along. If she plays hard to get, which I kind of expect from her, it'll be even more enjoyable when she finally gives it up. If she throws herself at me, either because she wants to avoid the complications, or as a way of getting at her mom - who she's never had much of a decent relationship with anyway - or because she actually wants me for real, I'll be the one making sure she doesn't get it that easily. Either way it's a win-win situation for me.

"Please, Daddy," Lottie simpers. "Please don't tell her."

I shake my head as I turn the baggy of weed around in my hands. "I don't know, Lottie," I say. "She has a right to know what her daughter gets up to."

"Come on," Lottie says. "You know she'll kill me. I'll be grounded for life. And it's not even mine."

I pause theatrically, making out that I'm thinking. "I can't," I say. "Not with something like this. If I decided not to tell her and then she found out I knew…"

"She won't find out," Lottie insists. "Only you and I know, and I'm not going to tell her."

I shake my head, suck air over my teeth and give her a deep, thoughtful gaze. *Those lips are so gorgeous*, I can't help thinking to myself, *I can't wait to see them wrapped around my dick.*

"I don't know, Lottie," I say again for emphasis. "This is kind of a big deal."

"Please," Lottie pleads, "I'll do anything."

"Huh," I say, pretending to think again. "You really don't want your mom to find out about this, do you?"

"She grounded me for a month and a half after Justin's party," Lottie says, flopping listlessly down onto the sofa next to me. "If she finds out I've been smoking weed, she won't let me out for the rest of the year."

"Alright," I say, "I won't tell her."

"Really?" Lottie says, her face brightening into a smile.

I nod. "But you've got to do one thing for me," I say.

"Name it," Lottie says. "I'll do anything."

I keep as straight a face as I can. "Well, first, I want you to suck my dick."

Lottie looks at me for a while and then breaks into nervous laughter. "Yeah, right," she says, shaking her head.

"Okay," I say, reaching for my cell.

"What are you doing?" Lottie asks.

"Calling your mom," I say, spinning through the contacts to find her number. When I get to it, I show Lottie.

"You can't do that," she complains.

I connect the call, and then put it on loudspeaker so we can both hear the rings. "I'm not kidding, Lottie," I say while I wait for her mom to pick up. "Either you suck my dick or I'm telling your mom about your drug habit."

Panic spreads across Lottie's face and it's clear she doesn't know what to do. Before she can answer, her mom picks up the phone.

"Hello?"

"Hey Trish, it's David," I say.

"Hey honey, is everything okay?" Trish says.

I look over to Lottie, bag of weed dangling from my hand. "Okay," Lottie says, "okay, okay, I'll do it."

"Is that Lottie?" Trish asks. "Hey Lottie, what's that you are going to do?" she adds.

"Hey Mom," Lottie says, angry eyes all over me. "Oh, it's nothing, we're just playing a game, that's all."

"Okay, that sounds fun," Trish says.

"I was going to say sorry for being rude to you earlier," Lottie says, her ability to improvise impressing me.

"Oh, okay," Trish says, taken aback. "That's very mature of you."

"Yeah, I just wanted to say that. So, okay, have fun tonight," Lottie adds.

"Okay, err, listen, I've got to go, everyone's heading in," Trish says.

"Okay, have fun honey, I love you," I say.

"Okay, see you later tonight," Trish adds, before she cuts off the call.

I put the cell phone to the side and place the bag of weed on top of it. "That was impressive," I say.

Lottie looks disgusted, but I know she's hamming it up. "I can't believe--" she begins.

"Oh come on Lottie, it isn't that bad. Something tells me you might even enjoy it."

"You're disgusting," she says, ramping up the theatrics.

"You know you are cute when you get angry," I say.

"What if I tell Mom?" she says, her face lighting up with the sudden thought.

"Tell her all you like," I say. "You'll have plenty of time to chat once you're grounded, not that she'll believe you anyway, the way that you've been flirting with me."

"Me?" Lottie protests, her cheeks reddening.

"You can't blame me," I say, my eyes going down to the peak in my trousers where my rock hard cock is already insisting it gets attention. "I'm just giving you what you want."

Lottie screws her face up in mock disgust, her eyes going quickly down to my crotch and back again, making out that she's noticing my bulge for the first time, the little liar. "I can't believe I'm doing this," she says.

"I'm still waiting, Lottie," I say.

Lottie sighs heavily, her eyes flitting from the swell in my sweatpants to my eyes and back again.

"You want me to call Mom again?" I ask, reaching for the phone.

"Fine," Lottie says sharply. "Take it out and I'll suck it, Jesus."

"That's better," I say. "You don't have to pretend you don't want to do it either," I add, going for the waistband to release myself. "I know what you're really thinking."

Lottie's eyes sparkle as I reveal my swollen dick. Even though she pretends to look away, she steals a long glimpse through parted fingers. Eventually she dares herself to look at me directly, unable to hide the reddening of her cheeks in delight. Lottie bites her lip, as though a starving child might contemplate a meal, and then looks up to me sheepishly.

"It's huge," she says. "How am I meant to--"

"Come here," I say, beckoning her across the sofa to me. "You know how to suck dicks, right?"

Lottie shakes her head.

"Then I'll show you. Here," I say, taking her hand and wrapping her fingers around the base of my cock. "You want to feel the weight of it first, so you know what you're dealing with. Like that," I add, shuffling her fingers up and down slowly to masturbate my foreskin over my swollen crown. "Then when you've got the size of it, you just move your lips to it, open up your mouth and push me inside."

"Okay," Lottie says, edging her mouth closer to my throbbing hard on. "I can't believe I'm doing this."

"You mean, you can't believe you're *finally* doing this," I say, moaning heavily as Lottie runs my meat past her lips and into the soft, moist warmth of her mouth. I close my eyes and lean back into the sofa as Lottie tightens her lips around my cock and begins to suck me clumsily, slurping away, nuzzling her tongue around my cock head randomly, clearly having no idea what she's doing. After a while she pulls me out and smiles up at me, proud she's pushed herself to finally do what I know she's been wanting to do ever since I moved in.

"Like that?" she asks.

"Like that's a good start," I say. "But I think it'll be better if you lose the skirt."

"No way," Lottie says, shaking her head defiantly. "The deal was for a blow job, nothing else."

"Come on, Lottie," I say. "Take off your skirt, or I'm going to have to tell Mom about the weed."

"Daddy," she pleads theatrically, clearly intent on putting up some kind of mock fight, while at the same time not willing to let go of my cock. Her tiny hand wrapped around my shaft, holding me, her step-daddy, tightly, matched with her clear inexperience makes me want to skip the build up and plough her straight away. The thing is, the teasing is just going to make the pay off so much better, so the longer I can string this out the better I know it's going to be.

"Don't make me call her," I say. "Come on, it's just a skirt. It's not like I've never seen your panties before. You can even keep your socks on if you want."

"Just the skirt," Lottie insists, "and that's it."

Lottie stands up, quickly unbuttons her skirt as though she might change her mind if she doesn't do it immediately, and let's it fall to the floor, stepping out of it casually and back to towards the sofa.

"Hey," I say, catching her. "Wait a minute. Let me see."

Lottie sighs, her hands on her hips. "There, okay?"

I can just about make out the outline of her pussy, a little ridge where her pubic bone pushes the fabric forwards prominently, a suggestion of an innocence I'm going to make sure I corrupt.

"Okay," I say, allowing her to come back to the sofa.

"One blow job and that's it, and you promise not to tell Mom," she says, resuming her position.

"We'll see," I say. "That depends on how well you do it."

Lottie rolls her eyes, but this time she doesn't say anything.

"Here," I say, leading her. "Kneel down on the ground. Like that you'll be able to suck me deeper."

"Okay," Lottie says, folding herself down onto the ground in front of me and reaching up again for my dick.

"Wait," I say. "Put your hands on your knees and open your mouth. "I'm going to show you how to do this properly."

Lottie shrugs, and then complies, her hands on her knees, her face tilted up to me, her mouth so wide open I can see down her throat.

"Tighter, Lottie," I say. "Make your mouth as tight as your pussy."

She rolls her eyes but doesn't say anything. This time she purses her lips together into a pout, the tiniest hole left between them.

"That's better," I say, guiding my dick towards her. "Now keep them like that, as tight as you can, my dick is going to do the rest."

I run the fingers of my free hand through her hair, resting them on the nape of her neck to counterbalance my weight as I move forward, and with my dick already on her lips, I begin to slowly push my way inside her. Lottie's eyes widen with a mix of mischievous pleasure and innocent enlightenment, and as I thrust myself deeper towards her throat I hear her moan encouragingly. I go as deep as I dare before pulling out, my hand now free so my dick can work on its own, my movement controlled entirely by my hips as I begin to fuck my teenage stepdaughter's mouth with my huge, throbbing dick.

"Like that is how you do it, Lottie," I say. "That's how you suck your daddy's dick."

Lottie nods, her mouth full of my meat. After a while I pull myself out entirely to let her gasp down a lungful of air.

"Is that better?" Lottie asks, her lips moist with saliva.

"That's better," I say thoughtfully. "Much better, but it still isn't quite right."

"Please don't tell Mom," Lottie says again, without prompting. "I'll keep going, just tell me what else I need to do."

"Alright," I say. "You know, it doesn't feel right that I'm standing here naked while you've still got your clothes on."

"No," Lottie says, shaking her head. "You said--"

"Come on, Lottie," I say. "It's only fair. Just take your top off for now. If I can see your tits it'll make this blowjob so much better."

She scowls up at me, pretending to be offended.

"Come on," I say. "Don't pretend that this isn't turning you on. I bet your pussy is soaking wet."

Lottie lets her mouth drop open in mock horror. "That's something you're never going to find out," she promises.

"You can't deny it forever," I say. "I've seen the way you look at me, and this is your perfect chance to get what you want. I don't know why you're pretending you're not interested."

"I'm not interested," Lottie says.

"Is that why sucking my dick is making you moan?" I say. "Is that why it's making your pussy so wet you can't wait to have me inside you?"

"Liar," Lottie says, but the way she says it just proves my point even further.

"I know how much fucking your stepdaddy turns you on," I say. "Come on, show me."

Lottie shakes her head, but then, as though she can't fight it anymore: "What if Mom finds out?" she says sheepishly.

"Who's going to tell her?" I say. "I'm not, you're not."

"We can't," Lottie says. "It wouldn't be right."

"No," I say, "but it'd be fucking hot."

"Will you tell her if I don't?" Lottie asks suspiciously, as though looking for an excuse to do what she's pretending she doesn't want to do. "About the weed."

"What choice will I have?" I say, shrugging. "You still haven't sucked my dick properly."

"I can't believe this is happening," Lottie says, a shy grin turning the corners of her lips up. "I can't believe--"

"It's not that difficult," I say, cutting in. "We go to your bedroom, we take off our clothes and I put my dick in your tight, wet, little pussy and fill you full of my cum. Don't deny you don't want it."

"I..." Lottie begins, her eyes going anywhere else but mine.

I take my finger and place it under her chin, matching her theatrics with my own, playing the game that makes my dick swell. "Tell me this doesn't turn you on."

"I can't," Lottie says, not entirely clear whether she's agreeing with me or telling me she can't fuck me.

"Then come with me," I say.

"Fuck," Lottie says, an exclamation of realization that could equally be posed as a question.

I smile, my eyes flashing with greed. The cat that got the cream. "Okay," Lottie adds. "Fuck, okay." She bounces to her feet, takes my hand in hers and guides me towards the stairs. "Let's do this before I change my mind," she says.

I follow her up the stairs, that ripe peach of an ass twerking perfectly as she goes, thick fatness of her pussy lips shaped by the cut and swell of her panties. Inside she hesitates momentarily, clearly unsure what to do. "I've never--" she begins.

"Take off your top and lie down," I say.

"What if Mom..." Lottie begins, doubt creeping in.

I watch her patiently, proudly. The admiration of a father and the desire of a lover. Real life has finally brought me to a place my imagination has dragged me to for months, and nothing feels better.

"Your mom is on the other side of the city," I say. "She's so far away she won't even be able to hear you come."

"I still can't believe..." Lottie says, her eyes going up to me. "How long have you known?"

"Take off your top," I say, playing it cool. "I'll do the rest."

"Mom would kill us if she knew," Lottie says, whipping her top off with the same speed she removed her skirt.

"It's the last thing she'd expect," I say. "I'm supposed to be your daddy, after all."

"I know," Lottie says, reaching for the clasp of her bra. "It's that part that turns me on the most."

"Wow," I say. "And I thought I had the measure of you."

Lottie looks at her exposed tits and then back up to me with a shy smile. "Not quite," she says. "Where would the fun be in that?"

Her tits are magnificent, pert and perfectly formed with thick nipples I could spend the rest of the evening chewing on. I make my way across the room towards her.

"If we're going to do this," she says, "we're going to do it properly."

I mount the bed and move towards her, pinning her body underneath mine until I'm bearing down over her. "Absolutely," I say, dropping in to plant a kiss against those perfect lips, which she opens upon request to allow my tongue inside her.

"You don't know how long I've been wanting to do that," she says.

"Denying it not working out for you anymore?" I ask.

Lottie shrugs. "It was working out fine earlier," she says.

I slide down her body slightly until my mouth is at the level of her nipples, and as I take each one in turn against my lips, Lottie arches her back in delight. "Fuck," she says again, "I'm so sensitive."

She pushes her weight into me, wrapping her legs around

my back and pulling my cock towards her pussy. Like this, and while she's still wearing panties, all I can do is rub against her, but it seems to be enough at the moment, and even with fabric between us I can tell how wet she is.

"I want you," Lottie moans as she tightens her grip against my skin and dots my neck with tiny little bites.

"You've got me," I remind her.

I slide down further, a line of kisses left like a trail along her torso, to pause briefly at the knot of skin that forms her belly button. "I'm going to fill you full of my cum," I remind her, before I dip my fingertips under her waist band and threaten to tear her panties right off her.

"I'm not on the pill," Lottie says, as though thinking out aloud. "Mom would kill us if you got me pregnant." She giggles a little as my fingers find sensitive, rarely touched skin, tingles flashing across her abdomen.

"Then don't get pregnant," I say, pulling her panties down slowly, desperate to reveal her teenage gash in teases. First the line of pubic hair, dotting her pelvis like dust, then the ridge of her pubic bone, next the swollen tangle of skin that hides her clitoris, her perfectly fat, perfectly shaved pussy lips, and the promise of innocence about to be claimed. So perfect she shouldn't be legal, so taboo I shouldn't be doing this. But I am, and I'm not going to stop now.

Lottie smiles at me shyly. She shrugs, as though apologising for being perfect. "To your taste?" she asks.

She's so hot she makes my head spin, so fucking horny my dick can't stop twitching.

"I told you," I say. "I told you I made your pussy wet."

Lottie giggles, her secret rumbled. "What can I say?" she admits. "I guess I'm only human."

I fold myself over her, hands and tongue tingling, unsure which part of my body I want to appreciate her with first. I dance my fingers along her thigh and she groans as I near her, huge smile spread out across crimson cheeks.

"Fuck," Lottie says, as I tease the tip of my finger between her gash, just to test how wet she is. "Oh fuck."

I push her legs wide, and watch her slit yawn open slightly, the pinkness of the meat inside her pussy as appealing to me as a red rag would be to a bull. "Did you shave your pussy for me?" I ask her as I probe her hole, keen to test her tightness.

Lottie moans. "I fantasized about this," she says. "I play with myself thinking about you."

"Oh yeah?" I ask, the tip of my finger teasing its way inside her. She's tight, but turned on, so she's not impossible to get inside. "Me doing what?"

"This," she says. "Fingering me, licking me, fucking me."

While I push more and more of my finger inside her, I reveal her clit with the fingers of the other hand and lean close to lick it.

"Fuck," Lottie complains, involuntarily clamping her thighs together. "Too sensitive," she warns, "you'll make me come."

I ease away, moving my tongue to the side to nudge up against her swollen nub instead. "Like this?" I ask.

Lottie nods, her breath peaking into little squeals. "Like that," she says.

"You taste good," I say, moving my tongue towards her hole and pushing it inside her against my finger. "Fresh."

"That feels so fucking good," Lottie says.

I tongue her for a while, my finger nudging her clitoris as I suck up her taste and make the most of the moment. When I feel like her groans are peaking too soon I pull away, keen not to let her have it all at once.

"Don't stop," Lottie complains. "Not yet."

"Come on," I say. "It'll feel better if you come with me inside you."

"You know we shouldn't," Lottie says, sitting up to look at me, my dick, and her tight, bald pussy.

"I know we shouldn't," I say. "That's why we're going to."

"Just a little," Lottie agrees, "put it just a little way inside me, just to feel what it's like, and then you have to pull it out okay? You can't come inside me, even if I want you to, you can't come inside me."

That bullshit act is back again, but I'm not going to fall for it. I know exactly what she wants me to do, even if she's trying to tell me the opposite. "I'm just going to give you exactly what you want, Lottie, you just tell me to stop if you don't want it," I say, already moving my dick towards her pussy hole. "Lift up your legs and hold your pussy open for me."

"I can't believe we're doing this," Lottie says again, like a stuck record.

"I know, right?" I say, my dick finally touching her pussy lips. "Finally."

"That feels so fucking good," Lottie wheezes, the words broken as I nudge my way to her entrance and begin to apply force to break my way inside her. "So fucking good."

She's tight, only because she's never done this before, but not tight enough I won't be able to insist my way inside her. I push on the back of her thighs to elevate her pussy even more and roll my hips forward.

"Mmmhmmm," Lottie urges, halfway between a moan of desire and a sigh of relief, as my crown breaches her hole and her pussy muscles begin to gather me inside her.

"Fuck me," I can't help but spit out. "Oh, fuck me, Lottie, that feels so fucking good."

"Are you inside me?" Lottie asks. "Are you really inside me?"

"Fuck, yeah," I say. "I'm inside you. I'm fucking you. We're fucking each other."

Lottie moans and sinks back into the bed, her outstretched arms sweeping against the blanket. "I never thought it would feel that good," she gasps, her words barely more than a whisper.

"You want me to pull out?" I ask rhetorically.

"No," Lottie says, shaking her head. "Not yet. Go deeper."

"If you insist," I say, letting gravity drop my weight and force my dick even further inside her.

"Now I know," Lottie whispers, "what it really feels like with you."

I'm not even fully inside her yet, but this feels incredible. The way her pussy muscles are grasping my shaft, feeding me into her, the way her skin flushes in patches of red, that innocent, dirty, mischievous, fuck-me-as-hard-as-you-can-and-cum-buckets-inside-me look she has in her eyes, the taboo of this, the age gap, the fact she's my step-daughter and she wants this just as much as I do, the way my dick makes her pussy swell as it pumps its way in and out of her, it's making my balls itch with urgency, my pulse race, sweat break out on goose pimpled skin, and bolts of pleasure run up and down my spine so fast I think I'm going to electrocute myself.

"Like that, Daddy," Lottie offers. "Just like that."

I fuck her as deep as our bodies will allow, and so deep she can't help but moan, and then I pull out slowly just so I can tease her, just so I can make her wonder every time I'm on my way out whether that's going to be the last thrust I give her, whether I'm going to make good on my promise, before I drop my weight again, roll my hips and drive my way back inside her.

She's trembling by the time we change position, moaning with deep guttural shards of breath that only serve to turn me on even more whether she means to or not. She's enjoying every minute of this, and there's nothing else that excites me more. I'm balls-deep in my wife's daughter, about as taboo a situation as you can possibly conceive of, and she wants me here more than anything else in the world.

We fuck doggy style while I finger her button-tight anus and my balls slap hard against her pussy lips, and I sit her on top of me while she rides my dick up inside her, both of us just about holding on. When I put her on her back again, this time her legs up on my shoulders to encourage my cock even deeper, I know I've pushed us both past the point of no return.

Lottie is the first to go, screaming so loudly and jerking involuntarily, I know it's upon her and about to hit her hard.

"Fuck, Daddy, fuck, oh fuck, I'm going to come," she says, the words spinning out of her mouth at about a million miles an hour.

"Lottie, if you come, I won't be able to hold on," I warn her, but it's already too late to bring her all the way back down.

"Fuck," she manages. "What if--? I can't get pregnant."

"You want me to?" I ask, barely holding it back myself, and certain she's not going to force me out of her. "The chances--"

"Fuck it," Lottie says, her chest rising and falling with heavy gasps. "I want you to come inside me. Fuck it. If you get me pregnant, so what?"

That's enough to send me right over the edge with no chance of returning, and as Lottie descends into her own hard-hitting, multiple orgasm, I feel my own about to explode around my body. Fucking Lottie and coming inside her is an absolute dream come true but to hear her say she wants me to fill her full of my come *and* make her pregnant, that she wants me to breed her, well that's just like heaven itself has opened up to me.

Lottie's legs jerk out, her skin bobbles with goose pimples, sweat clings tightly to her forehead and she screams in pleasure as it hits her, one wave after the next, her nipples thick and erect, her pussy throbbing and pulsating. "Fuck," she manages, clearly overwhelmed, a halfway mess of pure emotion and unadulterated pleasure. "I can't stop coming."

She pulls me into her, hands on my ass to hold me tightly against her body, no chance of pulling out even if I wanted to, and I come hard, thick robust streams of hot sticky cum, deep into my teenage step-daughter's pussy. I must ejaculate about six or seven times, before I collapse on top of her, my entire body tingly and sensitive, only to come again, when she shifts into a new position underneath me.

It is the best sex I've ever had without a shadow of a doubt, and perhaps the first time I've ever had a multiple orgasm. Lottie looks like she's enjoyed it too, like she might not even come back down from cloud nine.

"Fuck," Lottie says breathlessly, "that was, fucking hot, and fucking stupid." She pauses to giggle. "I can't believe you came inside me. We probably shouldn't have done that."

I have to wait a while for my breathing to return to normal before I respond. "Too fucking right we should have done," I say. "I've never come like that in my life."

Lottie giggles again, perhaps coming to terms with what we've just done and finding that laughter is the only way to react to it.

"Me either," she agrees. "I guess we'll probably have to do that again some time."

"What would your mother say?" I ask, rolling over to pull out of her, my dick still hard and showing no signs of going down. Lottie reaches for it to give me a squeeze, the taboo firmly broken, our roles changed, her inhibitions set to one side.

"I don't know," Lottie says. "Maybe I should tell her."

"Oh yeah?" I say, pulling her into me. "She'd kill me," I say. "She'd kill us both."

"She'd kill you more than me," Lottie says, "after all, you are supposed to be the responsible adult."

I can tell she's scheming, and I can't say I don't like it. "You're not going to tell her," I say.

"I might," Lottie threatens. "Of course, we could come to an arrangement."

She rolls herself on top of me expertly. "Oh yeah?" I ask.

"Yeah," Lottie says. "It'll be kind of our secret." She straddles me, rubbing her pussy against me dick suggestively. "Unless you want me to tell Mom, of course."

"You're something else," I say, impressed, turned on.

"Thanks," Lottie says with a beaming smile. "I think we should start straight away."

THE END
Get Access to over 20 more FREE Erotica Downloads at Shameless Book Deals

SHAMELESS BOOK DEALS is a website that shamelessly brings you the very best erotica at the best prices from the best authors to your inbox every day. **Sign up to our newsletter** to get access to the daily deals and the Shameless Free Story Archive!

A NIGHT FULL OF SIN - KIMMY WELSH

❦

My Step-Father Glen's coming to pick me up from my friend's party but while I wait for him the conversation turns sexual.

We poke fun at each other for still being virgins, with all of us claiming that we've had our first times already. As Glen pulls up my friends can't wait to tell me how much they have the hots for him.

Well tonight he's all mine. Glen and I slowly get onto the topic of sex too and soon he's showing me exactly what I've been missing! Read how he claims me – first time, hard and raw.

~

The party was winding down and I'd already called my Step-Daddy to come and pick me up. Mom was out of town so it fell on Glen to do the duties. He seemed pretty cool about it.

"How are you getting home?" Claire said as we sat in a circle on the front lawn.

"Glen's giving me a lift home," I said as quiet as I could, shifting my eyes over the group. There was a palpable silence and then a snigger.

"*Come and rescue me, Glen!*" one of the girls mocked and the rest of them started to guffaw. I turned red in an instant.

"Whatever," I said, waving a hand dismissively.

"*Take me home, Glen,*" Aubrey continued. "*Take me home and fuck me!*"

Claire gasped. "Aubrey! They're family!"

"Not really," Aubrey countered. "And besides, Glen's fucking hot."

That was something we could both agree on.

"I'd fuck him," she continued. "He'd have the night of his life!"

"You've never done it," Sara shouted. "You told me."

"I have," Aubrey said. "It's Amanda here that's the virgin."

She nodded in my direction again and I felt the scrutiny of the group on me.

"I've had sex before," I lied. "A bunch of times."

"Oh yeah? Who with?" Aubrey said.

"I don't remember *all* their names," I joked and thankfully the girls laughed.

Just then Glen's car pulled up and he flashed his headlights.

"There's your white knight," Aubrey said.

"See you later," I waved.

"Try not to accidentally fuck him," Aubrey shouted after, loud enough that I was sure Glen would hear.

I shot her a stern look and then smiled back at my Step-Daddy as I opened the door.

"What was all that about?" he asked as I sat down.

"Go," I said quickly, and Glen pulled off as my friends blew kisses at him.

I laughed and shook my head, bringing a hand to my forehead in disbelief.

"Oh, to be nineteen again," he said, rapping his hands on the wheel. He was smiling and seemed to enjoy the attention.

Glen had been my Step-Father for a couple of years now. Even though I was nineteen he still kind of felt like one of the family and I couldn't deny that Mom had really found herself a catch.

Glen was in his early forties, but there was something about him that was unmistakably hot. He had these green, piercing eyes that seemed both kind and dangerous at the same time. His hair was short and well groomed and he always seemed to have the perfect amount of stubble across his strong jaw.

I didn't mean to do it but I let out a frustrated sigh and the second Glen heard it he knew something was up.

"Everything okay?" he asked, glancing over.

"I guess," I said, in a way that told him the complete opposite.

"What's wrong?"

I huffed again. "Just my friends."

"What about them?"

"They keep making a big deal out of sex."

There was a moment's silence. I don't think Glen had anticipated a conversation like this on the way home.

"Do you think it's a big deal?"

"No. I don't know. I guess," I shrugged.

"What do they say?"

"They all joke about everyone being a virgin, but half of them haven't even done it themselves!"

"Have you?" he asked.

"Have I what?"

"Have you '*done it*?'"

I stared blankly ahead and wondered if I should spill.

"It's okay if you haven't," he said gently, and he placed a hand on my thigh.

I had on a pair of tight, white jeans and I could feel the heat of his hand through them. It seemed as though Glen really cared about me and moments like this were especially rare.

"It feels like time is ticking away," I said softly.

Glen laughed. "You're nineteen, not ninety!"

I smiled and looked over at him. Fuck, he was hot.

"How many times have you ... ?"

"I'm not sure that's a question my Step-Daughter wants answered," Glen said, looking over.

"What's it like?"

"You just won't quit, will you?" he said, laughing. "You really want to know?"

"Yeah," I said defiantly. "Tell me what I'm missing out on."

Glen's hands gripped the wheel tight. "It's amazing. Feeling the warmth of a woman's pussy sliding over your hard cock ... feeling how wet she is ... seeing her enjoy it. It's hard to describe. You're a girl too, so I guess it's different."

I was speechless. I wasn't expecting him to go into so much detail but as the words left his mouth I found my jaw dropping and my crotch dampening.

Glen looked over when I didn't say anything. I was kind of staring blankly through the windshield as my mind dreamt up all kinds of naughty images.

"Amanda?" he said, startling me.

"It sounds ... hot," I gushed, my shoulders shivering.

"It'll happen for you," Glen said. "You're an attractive woman."

"Really?" I asked, looking down at myself.

"Sure," he said, without missing a beat. "You've got a great body, pretty face, amazing personality. What couldn't a guy like?"

I was blushing now. Glen had never been so complimentary.

"Thanks, Daddy," I said, and it caused Glen to look over, forgetting the road for a second.

I'd never called him that before really, but I could tell in an instant that it was something he liked.

"What did you say?" he asked.

I pursed my lip. Maybe the opportunities to lose my virginity were closer to home than I thought.

"Daddy. Was that naughty of me?" I asked, playing the role of vulnerable young woman, suddenly.

"It just sounded ... funny."

"I can stop if you want ... *Daddy*," I said again, testing his nerve.

Glen's back straightened and he rolled his head on his shoulders.

"No, it's cool," he said, trying to compose himself.

I sat with my back against the door and stared across at him, wandering my eyes all over him as I began to exude this sexy confidence. All this talk of sex was making me hungry for it.

Glen's legs opened wider and he moved a hand to adjust himself. My eyes walked down his powerful chest and to his crotch, noticing the bulge in his pants that I was sure wasn't there before.

"Everything okay?" I asked back, flipping the tables on him.

I bit a finger in my teeth as I looked at him and when Glen looked over at me I made sure he saw me staring at his crotch.

"Just a little—*ahem*—excited."

"I can see," I said, and I felt the yearning inside me grow. My friends wanted to fuck Glen so badly—imagine if I beat them to it!

I slid closer to him and peered down at his crotch. He did a double-take and tried to concentrate on the road.

"What are you doing?" he asked, worried.

"Giving you a hand," I said, and I started to rub up and down along his thick, muscled thighs.

"It's not your hand I want," Glen said suggestively, and I felt a tremble run through me. It seemed far from an innocent remark. It felt like Glen *wanted* me to go further.

As my hand slid along his thigh I began to move it closer to his crotch, teasing a few inches closer to the bulge that was running down the inside of his leg.

The second I touched it Glen let out a breath and I could sense immediately that I was feeling something entirely different now. It felt stiff and alien, continuing along his thigh for an impressive amount of time before rounding off at the tip.

I rubbed along all of it and watched the expression in his face change from one of indifference to pleasure in a few seconds.

"Amanda, I'm not sure—"

"About what, *Daddy*?" I cooed seductively. "Should I stop?"

I continued to rub over him and his cock showed no sign of relenting. It felt long and hard and I wanted it. He let out a frustrated sigh but refused to finish his sentence.

I took it as a cue to continue and I popped open the button at the top of his fly. In the silence of the car I was sure I could hear his heart beating—or it could have been mine. I was so nervous but determined not to let it show. I wanted to be perfect for him.

I continued unfastening the buttons at the front of his pants until they were all undone. Beneath them sat his tight, white boxers and beneath those ... well, I was going to find out.

Glen shuffled again in his seat, only this time it seemed like he was moving for me. I suddenly had a greater vantage at his crotch and I seized the moment.

I rushed my hand down the front of his boxer-shorts and made a grab for the stiff appendage, pulling it out and marveling at the sight before me.

Glen's knuckles turned white as they gripped the wheel, but all I could do was stare at it. I moved my hand away and watched it for a moment as it stretched up the front of his t-shirt. It was thick and impressive, with powerful veins shooting up its length that caused it to twitch each time his heart beat.

"Well you can't stop *now*," Glen said, looking down at his cock and then to me.

I bit my lip and moved back to it, wrapping my fingers around it delicately as I held it.

"Just slide your hand up and down," he encouraged, guiding me through it.

My soft skin traced up his length and I curled my fingers tight around him to feel the heat of his dick. This was the closest I'd ever been to a stiff cock and I was determined to get even closer.

"That's right," he said softly, taking his hand off the wheel briefly to hold mine and move it over himself. "Just like that."

Glen set the pace and when he let go I kept it up, squeezing at the barrel and gliding from hilt to tip.

"Now put it in your mouth," he said, lifting his hand from the wheel so I could get in at him.

I shuffled closer and became excited in an instant. All of my wildest dreams suddenly seemed to be coming true.

I curled a lock of hair behind my ear and swallowed down my guilt, dropping my face to his lap and ogling his taboo length from inches away.

I licked my lips as I approached and thought of all the

friends who'd made fun of me. I couldn't help but let out a beaming smile as I approached, knowing that the next time I saw them I'd have some story to tell.

Glen's cock stood proudly at attention and I pointed it towards my lips, opening wide and sliding them close over the bulbous head of his crown.

He let out a huge breath as I pushed him past my lips, breaking the forbidden taboo and getting my first ever taste of cock in the process.

If Glen had felt big in my hand he certainly felt big between my lips and I struggled to keep my mouth open wide enough as I pushed him inside.

His hand rested on the back of my head and he scrunched my hair encouragingly. "That's right, Amanda," he said softly, with one hand on the wheel. "Suck Daddy's cock."

I pulled him from my mouth and looked down on his freshly drenched length. It somehow managed to look even more impressive strewn in my spit and I was already curious as to how it would feel when I finally put it inside me.

"Is that good, Daddy?" I said, swallowing and driving my fist over his slick cock.

"Perfect, honey," he said, glancing down. "Daddy's little slut."

I liked his new nickname for me but I felt there was more I could do to embody it. I pointed him back towards my mouth and plunged him inside again, becoming more adventurous and swirling my tongue around him as I drove him through my lips.

My head rocked down on him and my mouth held the base of his cock tight, sliding up and down it and spreading my spit all over him until he was glistening.

"That feels so good," he moaned, pushing his hips gently upwards and driving himself to the back of my throat.

I could feel my pussy begin to swell for him as I held him

in my mouth. He was rock-hard and aroused beyond measure and it was hot to know that it was all because of me.

"I want more, Daddy," I said, holding his cock close to my face and staring at it.

"How much more?" he asked, pushing his fingers through my hair.

"I want it inside me," I purred.

Glen jerked quickly and steered the car hard. I almost fell into the foot-well when he made the turn.

"Where are we going?"

"I know a place," he said. "Now keep sucking."

I was back on his cock in no time, driving him back inside me and rolling my tongue all over him. I licked all the way up him and circled around his sensitive head before putting the whole thing back in my mouth.

I tried to imagine all the porn clips I'd seen online and every word I'd heard my friends utter. I wanted to make things perfect for Glen and I wanted to show him I could be his naughty girl. It seemed as though Glen wanted it just as bad as I did.

"Here we are," he said, pulling up and shutting the engine off.

I dragged his cock slowly out of my mouth and looked over the dash. We were parked above the city overlooking it. The place seemed deserted. I'm sure I wasn't the first woman that Glen had brought here.

"What now?" I asked.

Glen leant over and kissed me softly.

"I'm going to show you what it's like," he said.

He opened the door and jumped out and I started to fantasize immediately. The excitement was so great that I was paralyzed by it.

"Coming?" Glen shouted, and I quickly sprang into action, trying not to let the smile run right off my face.

I jumped from the car and felt the warm, summer night's air on my skin. I skipped over towards Glen who sat on a bench overlook.

"It's magical," I gasped, looking down on the twinkling lights of the city.

"Ain't it just," he said, but Glen was looking at me instead. "Let me take a look at you."

He put his body close to mine and I reached down for his cock. To my dismay he'd tucked it back into his pants and I was fidgeting at his crotch all over again.

Glen was squeezing at my big tits and kissing my mouth and chin. My skin prickled with desire and as he kneaded my tits I ached for him even more.

He pulled my t-shirt over my head, throwing it across the back of the bench and looking me up and down.

"Damn," he said, unfastening his jeans and pulling out his cock.

I stayed a couple of feet from him and my eyes were instantly drawn to his sinful package as it sprang out of his pants all over again.

"Take your bra off, honey," he said, pumping his cock through his fist.

I reached behind my back nervously and unclasped my bra, dragging it off my shoulders and throwing it to the bench before folding my arms across my chest.

"No fair," he said, walking towards me. "Take your hands away."

Slowly I let them drop to my side and watched Glen's eyes twinkle in the moonlight as his pupils grew fat with desire.

"That's what I want," he said, and he pulled his t-shirt above his head.

As he did so the muscles of his stomach flexed and his pecs sprang out. His whole torso was ripped with muscle and

I began to melt when I saw it. I was suddenly realizing how lucky Mom was—how lucky *I* was—and my pussy surged with juices at the sight.

Glen stroked a hand over my tits before moving his face towards them and sucking on one of my nipples.

I giggled as it shot into his mouth and began to stiffen. Glen teased his tongue around it slowly and the shiver ran all the way down my back.

He brought his hands around me and squeezed at my tight ass, burying his face in my cleavage and kissing at my soft, pert breasts.

Glen took my hand and brought me over to the bench, standing only inches from me and putting his mouth close to mine.

"Ever had your pussy eaten?" he asked, and I struggled to keep from screaming with excitement.

"Never," I hushed, and I felt Glen's fingers slide down the front of my jeans and pull me towards him.

He snarled a kiss across my lips and our tongues entwined before he pulled away from me.

"Well I'm gonna show you that, too."

The button of my jeans popped open quickly and he slid the zipper down as he breathed another kiss into me.

His hands pushed down the front of my panties and soon I could feel his fingers creeping through the tuft of kempt hair that sat above my hot, virginal slit.

He nudged my clit as he rubbed me and it began to swell even further. I was a mess of lust when he finally began to yank down my pants.

I stood there and looked over the city as Glen sank to his knees, taking my jeans down my legs and dragging my panties with them. I felt the air drape over the wetness of my pussy as he helped me out of my jeans, then he pushed me back onto the bench.

I felt it's coolness on my ass as I sat on it and my legs flailed open. Glen was between them in an instant and his mouth was enveloping my pussy.

My eyes winced closed with pleasure and I let out a satisfied moan as his tongue searched up and down my wet flesh.

"Oh, Daddy!" I groaned, running one hand through his hair and another through my own.

Glen pushed his face onto my petals and parted them with his tongue, sliding down to my sticky honey-pot and stabbing inside my tight core.

"You taste so good," he said, sucking air through his teeth and then biting at my flesh.

"Don't stop, Daddy," I moaned, pushing my pussy onto him.

He was French-kissing my folds like a professional and the sensation was like nothing I'd ever felt. The furthest I'd ever gone was with my fingers and Glen's mouth certainly felt a whole lot different that that!

Glen continued for a couple of minutes and as he did so I felt the pleasure rising. It got so that I could barely contain it and I was screaming out at how good it felt.

"Don't stop, Daddy," I said, feeling my pussy swell for him and my clit stiffen. "Don't stop!"

It seemed he had no intention of stopping just yet and as his tongue tickled over me and he sucked my flesh between his teeth I could feel the orgasm building inside me.

My head rolled on my shoulders and I closed my eyes tight, sucking in a breath every so often and holding it so I could concentrate on the waves of pleasure surging from my pussy.

Glen slid a finger inside me and I cried out with glee, keeping his mouth on my clit before introducing another digit.

I felt my muscles clench around him when he pushed himself inside and pressed against my g-spot.

"Come for me," he said quickly before planting his lips back on me.

Glen didn't even need to say it, but when he did it felt like he'd granted me a special kind of permission.

Suddenly it was my *goal* to come, and each time I held my breath it felt as though I was one step closer.

My pussy began to swell and throb and I my vision swirled with color as his tongue kept its fantastic rhythm over my pearly stud. I squeezed at my tits and grunted at the approaching climax, feeling it flourish inside and wash over me like a baptism.

"Yes, Amanda," he cried. "Come for Daddy."

I began to writhe on the bench, unable to control my body as the orgasm claimed me and took over. When I exhaled it seemed to gain power, sending me thrashing in front of him.

Glen kept himself clasped on my clit, flicking his tongue over it until my pussy was so sensitive that I couldn't stand it being touched any more.

I pushed him off me and screamed with delight, clenching my legs closed and feeling my thighs twitch erratically.

"Fu-uck," was all I could muster, curling into a trembling ball as Glen watched, proud of himself.

I could hear him removing his pants but I wasn't yet ready to come back to the world. I was taking quick, calming breaths and centering my focus on the fading orgasm in an effort to commit it to memory forever.

The orgasm was like nothing I'd ever experienced. I think the taboo nature of the encounter was accentuating the sensations. It felt so right it could never be wrong, but I knew very few people would see it like that.

When my eyes finally opened it was to the sight of Glen's

big cock being passed through his fist. He was waiting for me.

"Ready?" he asked, curling a hand over his cock with purpose.

"I think so," I said, biting a finger and reawakening my body.

"On your knees," he said, pointing to the grass.

I moved quickly, keen to please him. I knelt to the floor and then fell forwards onto my hands, looking back at Glen and seeing him ogle my ass.

"Damn," he said, shaking his head.

"Like the view, Daddy?" I said, growing in confidence with each of his compliments.

"I like the taste," he said, dropping behind me and giving my pussy another kiss.

My eyes closed and I let out sigh of pleasure that rode on when I felt him tickle around my asshole. That was something that would have to wait, but to feel his tongue circle it like that certainly had me intrigued.

He was back on his feet behind me now and I turned to see him dropping down on me.

"Here it comes," he said, warning me.

I felt his thick rod gliding along my slick lips that were still covered in his spit, then he changed the angle of his cock and put it on my tight opening.

He pushed downwards and I felt the pressure build against my muscle. I winced with pain and it felt as though it would never relent, but Glen kept on regardless.

Suddenly I started to squeeze open gradually and his inches began to fill me, little by little.

"Daddy!" I screamed, then his cock plunged quickly inside me.

I grunted with pain as his size filled me in an instant. I felt full-to-bursting and the sensation was such that I thought he might have broken me.

I was taking quick, short breaths now as I tried to calm myself and I moved a hand to my pussy to assess the damage and check if this was really happening.

My finger teased slowly at my clit as if to relax myself, and then I ventured slowly down to feel at the taboo union of our flesh.

I made a V over his cock with my fingers and slid them back and forth over my pussy.

"Just a second, Daddy," I cried, struggling to compose myself.

Glen waited patiently. By now even the pulsing of his cock was threatening to make me scream out in pain, but gradually I began to relax around him and the pain slowly began to subside.

He pulled his cock out of me slowly, pausing each time I gasped before I could feel the bulbous crown threatening to pop out of me.

He moved himself back inside as he dropped his body, and after a moment the pervading sensation became one of pleasure.

"How does it feel?" he asked, sliding it with a slow rhythm through my tight lips.

"It feels good, Daddy," I called back to him.

Glen dropped over me and his body fell on my back. I took his weight each time he sank into me and began to wail out with pleasure as his thick slab of sinful flesh parted my lips over and over.

"Fuck me, Daddy," I grunted now, keen to see if he could give me more.

Glen didn't disappoint, quickly upping his pace so that his cock was ribbing its way through me faster than ever.

He squeezed at my tits and then fell back to kneel behind

me, gripping my ass and pulling it onto him each time he pushed forwards.

"Yes! Yes! Yes!" I cried, enjoying the slap of his hips against my butt. His cock was plunging so far inside me that I wondered how I was able to take it.

Glen let a slap down across my ass that caused me to clench around him and he stopped to enjoy the sensation.

"Oh, yes, baby," he sighed, rubbing each of my ass cheeks in circular motions as he looked down at his disappearing cock.

"Are you ready for me?" he asked.

"Ready?"

"For my cum," he said.

I barely had chance to think about it before my mouth was answering for me.

"Yes, Daddy," I cried, moaning and dragging my ass forward off him. He stayed put for the moment and clapped my ass back and forth along his dick, jerking through my lips.

"You want my cum?" he asked, squeezing my ass hard.

"I want it all," I begged. "Every last drop, Daddy!"

"That's my girl," he said, slapping my ass and resuming control.

He gripped my hips hard and drove into me faster than ever. The sensation of his cock was close to making me lose it all over again and I hoped Daddy could beat me to climax.

My tits shook on my chest and he clapped hard against me over and over as he pushed himself to release.

"I'm close, honey," he warned, snarling and looking down at my ass.

"Do it," I dared. "Shoot it inside me!"

He continued for a few moments longer, his breath racing as it became more audible. I could feel the arousal in the stiffening of his dick, causing it to feel like slick rock as it surged through me.

"Here it comes," he gasped. "Here it comes."

There was a sense of urgency in his words and I braced myself for the grand finale.

"Give it me!" I yelled, just as he froze at his most frantic.

There was a silence and I looked back to check if he was okay, seeing his eyes closed tight and then watching him let out a long breath.

"Oh, Amanda," he sighed, and then I felt the first thick, hot lashing of his cum bursting inside me.

I rocked back on his cock and fed his seed inside me. There was something hot about Glen's raw cock coming in my virginal pussy. The thought of him impregnating me was dangerous, but it somehow made the moment even more memorable.

"Come inside me, Daddy!" I cried again, feeling him throbbing out the hot ropes of his love.

Several more thick jets of cum flashed up into my core until it was brimming from my pussy. As Glen pulled himself out of me and pushed his seed deeper, his cum ran out around his dick, dripping off me to the floor.

I had no idea how I'd explain myself if Daddy's seed took root, but for now I didn't care. All that mattered was how good it felt having him come inside me. There was something special about making him climax, as though my pussy was made for him.

I rocked back on him and made sure I got everything. I felt as though I'd earned it.

"Yes, Daddy," I purred, looking back at him with lust.

"Fuck, Amanda," he gasped, falling out of me and sitting back on his ass. "That was incredible."

His eyes were gasping open in shock, as though he'd just awoken from the wildest dream.

"I know!" I said, crawling over to him and kissing his face. "You're amazing."

I kissed him again and again as he gasped in air, trying to bring himself back to a sense of normalcy. Something told me that things might never be normal again.

I fell against him and rested my head on his chest, listening to his heart beat as I fantasized about telling my friends what I'd done. I didn't care if they believed me now.

THE END
Get Access to over 20 more FREE Erotica Downloads at Shameless Book Deals

SHAMELESS BOOK DEALS is a website that shamelessly brings you the very best erotica at the best prices from the best authors to your inbox every day. Sign up to our newsletter to get access to the daily deals and the Shameless Free Story Archive!

NOT A LITTLE GIRL ANYMORE - ABIGAIL BLACK

Christy is tired of her step-father's stupid rules!
Yes, she can do what she wants in college, but who wants to wait seven months? That's an eternity.
After he chastises her for sneaking out, she decides to get even. She plans to handcuff him to his bed and run away, but when she realizes how helpless he is, her plans change.
What happens when Christy teases him? What happens when she pulls the covers away to reveal a very naked, very excited step-father? What happens when the man of the house cannot resist her?
Innocent, untouched Christy is about to go too far.

"Yes! He's asleep!" Christy grinned when she saw that her step-dad's patrol car was still in the driveway and the house lights were off. She'd snuck out the window as soon as she could because she was sick of having a 10pm curfew even after she'd turned eighteen last week. She'd checked out the local party scene, but it was just the same jerks from high school.

Christy was able to open the door and sneak into the living room without a sound, but the overhead light clicked on just as she was closing the door. *Busted!*

"Exactly where the hell have you been, young lady?" Her step-father's voice was hard, and Christy flinched despite herself. Even though she usually would beg for forgiveness when she was caught misbehaving, this time she decided to counter-attack.

"I went out. I'm eighteen, so I can do that now."

Brad laughed. "Not as long as you live in this house, you don't. My house, my rules."

Christy felt her face growing red. "Brad, everybody else is out having a good time. I'm not a little girl anymore. I should be able to go out and enjoy myself."

Brad shook his head. "There are ways to have a good time without crawling all over town and getting into God knows what kind of trouble. In seven months, you'll be in college and can stay out as late as you want, but I promised your mother that I would take care of you, and that is exactly what I plan on doing."

Christy flinched again. Her mother had died just over a year ago, and Brad always used that line against her. The shitty thing was, it usually worked.

Before Christy had a chance to respond, Brad stood up. "Now get to bed. We'll talk about your punishment tomorrow. Right now, we both need to get at least *some* sleep." He didn't wait for her answer but turned his back on her and started toward her bedroom.

That pissed Christy off. "Whatever!" She stormed to her room and slammed the door.

Christy paced around her bedroom for several minutes before flouncing onto the bed and punching her pillow. It just didn't do the job. She wanted to punch the hell out of that asshole down the hall. She wanted to move out, but she didn't have anywhere to go. *Seven months, and then I'm free.* But that meant seven months of the same old shit.

Christy stood up and went to her dresser to pull out something to wear to bed. She chose a thin, blue tank-top and a matching set of panties and then shucked off what she was wearing. *If only I could prove to him that I'm not a little girl anymore.* As Christy thought this, she saw herself in the mirror and paused. *Anyone can see that I'm not a little kid. All they have to do is look.* Sometimes Christy thought that Brad did know that she was grown, especially in the mornings when he came out of his bedroom for breakfast. She wasn't sure, but she thought that he looked at her differently than he had a few months ago.

Maybe that's how I convince him. I can force him to see that I'm grown. Christy smiled and finished dressing. A few moments later, she stood outside his door and listened. Brad's breathing was deep and slow, not snores, but relaxed enough that she was sure he was asleep. Holding her breath, she cracked open the door.

From the light that filtered in through the blinds, Christy could see Brad stretched out under the covers. Trying to decide what to do, she looked around and spotted his uniform laid out on a chair. Christy snuck over and gently lifted his handcuffs. Grinning, she looked back at him. One quick snap, and she could cuff one of his hands to the rail of the bed. Then she could mess with his head a bit, throw him the keys, and run like hell to her bedroom before he could free himself.

Christy held her breath again and crept up to him. *He's really asleep.* Christy snapped one of the cuffs around the rail, took a deep breath, and snapped the other cuff onto his wrist before leaping out of reach. Brad woke up the instant the cold cuff hit his wrist, and he almost managed to grab her as she jumped out of the way.

"What the hell do you think you're doing? If you don't uncuff me right now, I'm going to whip your ass!"

At first, she had just planned on trapping him so she could lecture him and then threaten to pack her stuff to move out, but now that he was stretched out in front of her, she started having other ideas. Maybe it wouldn't hurt to torture him just a little bit first.

Christy cocked her head at him and smiled. "I'm sick of you thinking I'm still a little girl, so I thought I'd show you what you apparently aren't able to see. I am grown." She ran her eyes all the way down him and then all the way back up again. He *was* hot. One of the reasons that she hadn't been interested in the boys in her class is that she saw every day what a grown man looked like, and it wasn't any of them. Brad's muscles jumped as she ran her eyes over them, and when she finally got to his eyes, they were wide in panic, and maybe something else.

"Wait a minute. What are you thinking?" His voice was level, just like it was when he was trying to prevent a crook from doing something stupid, but his face was starting to flush. Christy held eye contact with him, but she was pretty sure that his face wasn't the only place the blood was starting to rush.

"Oh, I don't know. Let's start by you staying quiet and paying attention to me." Christy started backing up toward the foot of the bed, but she paused long enough to grab the covers and yank them off Brad's lower body. Her breath caught. He was naked under the blankets, and she definitely had his full attention.

Brad jerked his free hand down to cup his hard-on, but as big as his hand was, it wasn't enough to block her view. "Christy, you don't want to do this. Just throw me the key, and we'll forget any of this has happened." Christy only half-heard Brad's voice because blood was starting to pound in her ears, and she felt her own face flushing.

She drew a deep breath and continued to back to the foot of the bed where she knew they would both have a good view. Part of her wished she could back out and forget this, but she knew that if she stopped now, he'd never see her as grown. Christy forced herself to calm down and keep going.

"No, Brad. You seem to think that I'm a little girl, and I'm sick of it. I am a grown woman, and it's time you faced facts." For a second, Christy thought about how much she sounded like her mother, but she pushed that thought away, along with the one about how this was her mother's husband naked in front of her.

"Look at me, Brad. Does a little girl have breasts like these?" Christy ran her hands over her light blue tank-top and then cupped her breasts. She squeezed them gently and was surprised at how good it felt to touch herself. Her nipples hardened, so she stroked them a little bit. *God, that feels good!* Christy closed her eyes for just a second while she played with her nipples. When she opened them, she saw that Brad's mouth had opened and he had shifted his hand around the shaft of his thick cock.

"Yeah, Brad, I know you. You don't jerk off to little girls, do you? You're only interested in grown women. Would you like to get a better look at them, Brad?" His only response was a quick nod. It looked like he was holding his breath.

Christy pinched her nipples to make sure they were plenty hard before she slipped her hands down to the bottom of her tank-top. She crossed her arms and pressed them against her breasts to make them stand out more. Brad's breathing started again, and he was practically panting. Christy smiled and slowly lifted the top off of her body. Brad moaned and started stroking his cock again. Christy lowered her eyes and watched him, trying to get a sense of what it was that he liked. He had a firm grip on the shaft, and he pulled his hand up his length before cupping the head with his palm and grinding into it and then sliding back down the shaft again.

Christy realized that she was getting wet just watching him.

She cupped her breasts again and started playing with her nipples. Brad shifted his hips and ground harder into his palm. Christy slid one of her hands between her legs and felt the juices soaking into her panties. She slipped one finger under them. It felt good, but she really couldn't reach anything standing there. She bit her lip nervously and decided to join Brad on the bed. It was a risk, because he was so lanky that he could kick her if he wanted to, but given the look in his eyes, she didn't think that was what was on his mind.

Christy drew a deep breath and decided to move forward. She hadn't ever done anything like this before. Honestly, all the guys at her school were terrified of Brad, and compared to him, they really were just kids. They were too scared to make a move on her, and she had never really been interested in any of them.

Brad was a different story. She was realizing that she didn't want to just mess with Brad's head. She wanted to fuck him.

"You know, I think you're starting to get the idea that I'm not the little girl you seem to think I am. But I don't think I like watching you jack off like this." Christy slipped her panties off and moved slowly back toward the bed. Brad froze and watched her mount the bed. Reluctantly, he removed his hand from his cock and grabbed his other hand, locking his fingers together and watching to see what she did next.

Christy knelt between his feet with her knees apart. She touched her breasts, lightly at first but then more firmly, kneading them for a few seconds before squeezing her nipples again. Her breath was coming faster, but she still hadn't done the things that she wanted. Holding onto her left breast, she slid her right hand down her stomach and between her legs. When her fingers hit the wetness she found down there, her whole body spasmed.

Jesus, is this how it feels?! She had never touched herself like this, afraid she'd get caught.

Christy closed her eyes again and started exploring the slippery area for the first time. Her body kicked again when she hit the hard knot at the top of her slit. Forgetting about Brad, Christy rolled the knot under her fingers, soaking it with the slick juices that covered her pussy. Spreading her legs wider, Christy rolled back onto her heels and pumped her hips as she worked one hand against her hips and the other against her nipple. A weird tightness was starting to build inside of her, and she moved her fingers faster, afraid that the feeling would go away if she slowed down. When her first orgasm hit her, she cried out and almost passed out it felt so good.

In a voice that sounded too much like a little girl, Christy looked up with bleary eyes at her step-father. "Is it supposed to be like that?"

Brad laughed at her confusion, "Yeah, when you do it right. But, little girl, if I don't get some relief soon, I'm going to explode."

For some reason, Christy didn't mind it this time when he called her "little girl." Christy cocked her head to give him a little girl smile. "Well, *Daddy*, what do you want me to do?"

"Why don't you start by uncuffing me?"

Christy thought about it for a second before shaking her head. "I don't think I want to do that yet." She was afraid of what was going to happen once she gave him the key. She wanted to be sure she could at least get into her bedroom and lock the door before he got loose, maybe even get to the car. She hadn't really thought through what was likely to happen once he got free.

"In that case, why don't you see what you can do to help me out?" He cut his eyes from hers to his cock. Christy licked her lips and slid up from the foot of the bed to between his knees. Brad's cock was hard, and his balls were tight against his body. The area seemed darker than the rest of him, and a vein ran down the length of his cock.

Christy thought she could see it throb from his pulse. Even though she had been bold a minute ago, she had no idea what to do. Finally, she stretched her hand out and gently touched the head. Brad's breath came out ragged, but he didn't say anything. Christy glanced up at him and then back at his cock. She stroked it, running her fingers from one side of the head to the other.

"Oh, God, yes." Christy jumped at his voice. She smiled at his reaction. Curious, she traced a finger around the head, following its edge in a circle before it rose and then fell in an upside-down V. Christy thought about what was supposed to happen next. She leaned down and sucked gently on that area, just using her lips. Her tongue brushed against it, and she tasted salt. She lapped at it with her tongue while Brad moaned again.

Christy wiggled a bit closer to get a better angle on what she was doing. Mainly it was to give her time to figure out what she was supposed to do.

Brad had been so strict that she was having to figure out what most girls had known for years by the time they had reached her age. All she knew was from glimpses of movies and locker room talk from some of her more mature classmates.

She decided that she should lick the head while she stroked the rest of his cock. She slid her hand down his length while she licked the top of the head in short strokes, just like she did when she and Brad went to the ice-cream shop.

Brad lifted his hips, pushing his cock harder against her mouth. Christy knew she couldn't take in all of him—he was huge!—but she opened her mouth wide and took the head into her mouth.

Brad raised his hips and tried to push deeper into her mouth, but she shifted backward every time he pushed forward even though she kept his head in her mouth and kept licking. She found his slit with her tongue and tried to slide the tip of her tongue inside. Her hand kept moving on his shaft the whole time she licked and sucked, but she decided to go further down and play with his balls for a while.

"Easy, easy! God that feels good!" Christy grinned, and she felt her spit dribbled from the edge of her mouth onto his shaft. Drawing a deep breath, she opened her mouth wider to take more of him into her. She took the first few inches into her mouth before sliding back off to try to catch her breath. *I can't believe I'm doing this! I'm blowing my step-father!* Christy knew that she shouldn't even be here, but she didn't want to stop now that she'd come this far. She wanted more!

Ok, Christy thought, *what can I do now?* She wanted to seem experienced, but she had no idea what she was doing.

Christy's tongue brushed against the thick vein, and she decided to try tonguing that for a while. She rocked gently up and down on the few inches she'd been able to swallow, and Brad had rewarded her efforts with more moans. She decided to try to slide further down his cock, but she tightened her grip on the shaft and started working it just in case she had to pull back. She went a bit further down the shaft with her mouth, sucking and lapping the vein with her tongue.

Brad's hand settled on the back of her head and he gently pushed her further down his cock.

Christy's eyes widened.

What if I can't take anymore? What if I gag? What if I can't breathe? Panic set in and Christy started pushing hard against his hand trying to get away. When he released her, she came off his cock with a loud slurp.

"What's wrong? You were great!" Brad's balls were screaming at him to keep going.

"I couldn't breathe! I think I was choking!" Christy's voice had once again shifted to that of a little girl.

"I'm not going to hurt you or let you choke. You just need to practice how to breathe." Brad stroked his step-daughter's hair even though what he wanted was to finish up inside her mouth. "Do you want to let me go now so I can help?"

Christy bit her lip again, making her look younger than her eighteen years. She really wanted to know what it was like to suck him off, but she was afraid of how huge he was. "I don't know. You're so big!"

Brad grinned at her. "I'm going to teach you how good it feels to have this inside of you. Just let me go and I'll take care of you, baby."

Christy almost gave in, but she still wasn't sure what he'd do once he was free. Besides, she wanted to prove to him that she was grown, and freaking out over a blow-job wasn't the way to show him that she wasn't a scared kid.

Taking a deep breath, she shifted out of his arms and back to his cock. She licked her lips and took his head back into her mouth. This time, she wrapped both of her hands around his cock and worked this shaft as she sucked and licked his head and the top of his shaft. She flicked her tongue around the base of his head and lapped from the edge to his slit. She tasted something different leaking from his slit, salty but something else too. Brad's breathing started coming faster, and he gently pumped his hips against her mouth.

She slipped a little further down her step-father's shaft but rode higher again to catch her breath before sliding back again. Christy wanted to push down a little bit further each time, but she wasn't sure that she could make it all the way to the base. While her mouth worked its way up, down, and along his shaft, her hands worked along the base.

Christy was getting more of that new flavor, and Brad's breathing was coming in gasps now. He tightened his body hard against her and froze. Not knowing what else to do, Christy sped up and forced herself to take more of her step-father's cock down her throat. Brad let out a cry and Christy had to swallow as hard as she could to keep from getting sprayed all over her face. When his balls had finished emptying into his step-daughter, Brad reached out to stroke her hair and face before tugging on her shoulder to draw her onto his chest. Christy felt triumphant. She hadn't freaked out, and she had swallowed every drop.

Brad didn't say anything for several minutes, just stroked his stepdaughter's hair and thought about how good it was to get his cock sucked after going without for so long. He finally nudged her to see if she was awake. "Hey, look up here." When Christy did, he leaned in and kissed her, first just a gentle kiss like any father would give his daughter, but then more heated. Brad slid his tongue into his stepdaughter's mouth and was happy when she opened up to deepen the kiss.

It had been a long time since he'd held someone her age, and her young body was fit and fine. Given her reaction to the blowjob, Brad suspected that his stepdaughter was still a virgin, although how the hell that was possible was beyond him. If he had his way about it, this girl that he had raised for the past six years wouldn't be a virgin much longer.

Brad pulled out of the kiss. "Listen, why don't you get the key and let me loose. There are some things that I would love to show you."

Christy didn't hesitate this time. Even though she'd planned on throwing him the key and then taking off before he could get loose, she had decided to stick around to see what was going to happen next. Brad watched her tight ass as she slid off the bed and bent to retrieve the key to his cuffs.

As soon as the band popped open to free his wrist, Brad grabbed his stepdaughter and flipped her onto her back underneath him, pinning her arms as he did so. Her eyes widened as she realized that she was as trapped as he had been moments before. Brad shifted to that she could feel his hard cock pressed against her thigh. "I think I told you that I was going to show you how good it was to have something this big inside you. You didn't think I was meaning just your mouth, did you?"

When Christy didn't say anything, Brad continued, "Are you going to be a good little girl and let your stepfather show you what it's like?"

Christy just nodded.

Brad grinned. "Good girl."

Brad lowered his head to her firm, young breast and took her nipple into his mouth, first mouthing it but then tonguing and finally sucking it. Christy squirmed under him. Brad let go and looked up at her. "Are you ok?"

"Uh-huh." Christy blushed. "It feels really good."

"If you like that, you're really going to like what's coming." Brad massaged one breast while sucking the other, and he smiled when he heard Christy's breathing increase. He shifted his mouth from her breast and moved slowly down her stomach, kissing as he went. When he finally reached her hips, he spread her legs to gain access to her wet slit. Christy froze and watched to see what he was going to do next.

"Do you want your Daddy to show you what it's like to have a grown-ass man take care of you?" Christy just nodded. Brad grinned and lowered his mouth over the top part of her privates. Christy bucked off the bed and his lips settled on the hard knot of her clit. Brad took turns sucking and tonguing it while his stepdaughter moaned beneath him.

Reflexively, Christy spread her legs open even further which gave Brad better access with his mouth and his fingers. Still sucking her clit, he brushed his fingers against her opening. Christy moaned even louder. Moving gently, Brad massaged against her pussy, smearing her slick juices up and down her crack. Christy started pushing up against his hand, encouraging him to keep going.

Brad lifted his head again, and Christy cried out in disappointment. "You want me to stop?

"Nnnnoooo, God, No!"

Brad's grin lit up the bedroom. "That's my girl!"

He started tonguing her clit again, but this time he gently pushed one finger inside her, moving it gently to encourage her to open up even wider. Christy felt the same tightness as before building up in her stomach and she pumped harder against his hand and mouth. Within seconds, another wave of orgasms hit her, and she screamed even louder than before.

Brad didn't slow down but pushed deeper inside until he felt resistance against his finger. *WTF!?!? A Virgin!?!?* Brad knew that Christy hadn't had many opportunities to mess around, but it had never occurred to him that she might still be a virgin. And knowing this made his balls hurt even more.

Brad felt Christy shudder and knew to back off long enough to let her body get over the post-orgasm tenderness.

He shifted up in the bed, staying between her legs but where he could kiss her.

"You doing ok?"

He smiled at the dreamy look she gave him.

"I'm glad. Are you ready to try something else?"

"Uh-huh." She sounded like a little girl again.

"Are you sure?"

"Yes."

Brad reached down and stroked her again, making sure she was ready for him. He teased her opening with the tip of his cock until Christy started moving in time with his motions. It was killing Brad to take his time with this, but he wanted his little girl to love every second of this, and he knew that taking him in was going to hurt, no matter what he did to prepare her.

Christy was about to come out of her skin. Brad's size scared her, but she was going to go crazy if he didn't get on with it. When he finally shifted onto her, she thought that it was going to happen, but he kept teasing her and driving her crazy. Everything he did felt amazing, but her body was screaming for her stepdad to finally pop her cherry.

She could tell that the head of his cock was in the right place, but he kept brushing it against her instead of pushing on in. Christy started grinding harder against him and rocking hard to try to get him inside of her.

It was Brad's turn to moan. His baby was killing him. He tried to decide the best way to do this, but she was making it impossible to think at all. With Christy moaning underneath him, he slammed into her, popping his girl's cherry and stretching her wide with his thick cock.

OMG! Christy had never felt something that hurt so bad but still felt so good. It was like her insides were being ripped apart but it also felt better than anything she had done. Brad froze and waited for his stepdaughter, but he didn't have to wait for long. She shifted her hips and pushed against him.

"Baby, are you ok?"

Christy nodded and rocked her hips again. She didn't have to say anything more. Brad pulled back and slipped in again, speeding up as his stepdaughter joined in the rhythm he laid down. Christy wrapped her legs around his waist and lifted her hips, which seemed to help her take him in. Pretty soon she had forgotten all about the pain.

She heard Brad's breathing getting faster, and she knew that he was getting close to shooting his load. Christy moaned as he hit something deep inside her. It was at that moment she realized that she could get pregnant.

The thought of having a baby with the only man she truly loved... What felt like a million emotions bubbled up inside her. She wasn't a little girl. He'd made her a woman.

This time her orgasm hit without any warning, and she cried out hard. Her stepfather didn't slow down but pounded against her harder until he cried out too as he pumped his load into her.

Christy smiled as she felt him twitching inside of her. And she wanted every drop as deep inside her as possible.

Brad smiled down at her and stroked her hair before leaning down and kissing her. He pulled out slowly, and Christy realized she was throbbing from all the pounding he had done. She was just about to shift over to make room for Brad beside her when he grabbed her by the wrists and flipped around so she was over his knee. Christy squealed like a little girl. Just as the first sharp but playful slap landed on her ass, Brad reminded her, "I think I promised you that I was going to spank you, didn't I?"

THE END

Get Access to over 20 more FREE Erotica Downloads at Shameless Book Deals

SHAMELESS BOOK DEALS is a website that shamelessly brings you the very best erotica at the best prices from the best authors to your inbox every day. Sign up to our newsletter to get access to the daily deals and the Shameless Free Story Archive!

MY DAUGHTER, MY WIFE, MY NEW LIFE - ZOE MORRISON

Sean realizes that sometimes a new life needs redefining an old relationship.

Sean watched his step-daughter leap up the stairs and smiled. Morgan had just turned eighteen and was more excited than ever. He hadn't asked her what she wanted, but he would get what she needed -- his job had made him independently wealthy, and they both lived comfortably.

Before his eyes, Morgan had blossomed into a lovely young lady. She was tall and slender, with small but firm breasts -- and a butt you could bounce a quarter off of -- as well as long legs that seemed to go on forever. But the parts of her he liked best were her engaging smile and deep green eyes. As he thought about Morgan's smile, he was reminded of her mother who had passed away three years ago.

SEAN WALKED through to the game room of their modest house, and racked up a game of pool to just shoot some balls along; something he did when he needed a distraction. As he sank the last red solid, Morgan came in, and she immediately had his full attention.

She was dressed in a blueberry colored camisole over some jeans so tight they looked painted on, making her beautiful ass extremely pronounced even more so than usual. Sean shook his head as he knew he shouldn't be thinking about his daughter that way, but it again reminded him of his wife, as both women looked so alike.

She picked up the second cue and took the next shot. In doing so, she bent over and Sean felt an uncomfortable swelling in his pants as he was looking at that beautiful butt for the second time in as many minutes.

Clearing his throat, Sean sat down to try and hide the growing bulge in his crotch.

"What did you want for your birthday, sweetie? You can have your friends round if you want."

Morgan paused and looked up at him.

"Actually, Daddy, I was wondering if I could spend it with you?"

"Me? I'm an old man, sweetie, and it's your special day."

Morgan turned and leaned against the table, her eyes wide and shining with happiness.

"Exactly. That's why I want to spend it with you; make it a special daddy-daughter occasion."

"Okay. How?"

"Could you take me out for dinner? Somewhere classy?" she asked.

Sean gazed at his beautiful baby girl-woman for a moment, then nodded. He had a friend who owned a high-class restaurant in town, so he could easily arrange it.

"Sure honey." He smiled. "It's your day, whatever you want."

Morgan's pretty face split into a beaming smile.

"Thanks Daddy!" she giggled, jumping onto his lap and flinging her arms around him.

Despite enjoying the cuddle, Sean was all too aware of the erection in his trousers that -- due to her tight jeans -- Morgan could probably feel digging into her ass. She kissed him on the cheek and ran from the room.

Sean sighed, glad that his erection could finally start to subdue. Picking up the phone, he rang his friend. It was answered after two rings.

"Hey Sean. What can I do for you?"

"Can I get a table for two tonight?"

"Sure. There was a cancellation earlier so you can have a booth."

"Thanks. I owe you one," Sean laughed. There was a sudden commotion on the other end.

"Gotta go man. See you later," his friend said quickly and hung up.

∼

MORGAN LAID on her bed conflicted. She had felt her daddy's erection, and she knew it was because of her. It both shamed her -- she knew a daughter shouldn't feel that way about her father, even if technically it was her step-father -- but it also aroused her knowing her father found her sexy enough to get a hard-on.

She had asked her father for a meal alone for a reason, but she knew she risked alienating him completely. The only way she would find out was to talk to him, but it was a thought that scared her.

She didn't want to lose him, but she needed to be honest with him.

The thought of his bulging pants, however, was beginning to turn her on right where she lay on the bed. Very slowly her hands inched towards her skin-tight jeans and unbuttoned them as she simultaneously rolled over onto her back. She lightly pushed her hand down into her jeans while her other had snaked its way up to her breast and underneath the camisole and bra she was wearing. As her body was starting to react to her own manipulations of her hard nipples and even harder clit, she was imagining her daddy on top of her going in and out of her little cunt the way she heard the girls at school talk about so much. The more and more she thought about what he looked like naked, her finger speed was increasing almost whipping her knob silly while her hands on her tender nipple were twisting and pulling it raw. She could feel the orgasm approaching. She knew it was close and by now she couldn't stop it even if she wanted to but by no means did she want to. She was right at the threshold… just a little more… and… release.

As her breathing regulated and her heartbeat slowed down, she realized she had needed that to take the edge off for what she hoped would be a promising night but could also go horribly wrong if she had miscalculated. She felt as if she were standing at a precipice and her only option was to jump; no turning back at this point.

She took a deep breath, sighed, and then went back downstairs.

∼

MEANWHILE SEAN WAS GOING through his own baptism by fire. Seeing how Morgan's body had developed and how much she looked like his late wife, coupled with her very affectionate maneuvers, had awakened a fire in him that he had not dealt with in quite some time. He decided that he too needed something to take the edge off just so he could continue to see his daughter as his daughter and nothing else.

Leaving the game room, he went to his room and decided to take a shower, a cold one to quench some of the feelings he was feeling. He cut the shower on and once the water was ice cold, stepped in. Although he didn't really feel he needed a shower, he grabbed the soap nonetheless and started to rub his body with it.

In no time flat his thoughts were of Morgan again and visualizing her hands were the ones running up and down his body instead of his own. The more and more he thought of her touching him everywhere, while he in turn did the same thing to her, his hands began to make their way down to his manhood, which was by now sticking out in front of him like a beacon pointing the way straight to hell if he didn't stop these thoughts. His hand reached his cock and like the old pro he had become since becoming a widower, began pulling expertly with just enough pressure to make him close his eyes and give in to the mood.

His other hand reached under to cup his balls and he began to alternately massage and tug on them ever so gently. It didn't take long. In a few moments he felt the boiling deep within his balls so he opened his eyes and looked down to see the first spurts of cum on the head of his dick. He closed his eyes again and as Morgan invaded his thoughts once more -- the small firm tits, the tight ass, and those legs he could easily see wrapped around him -- his cock started to jerk in his hand and proceeded to splatter the walls of the shower with wasted seed that he and Samantha had hoped would bring them another child one day. All of a sudden, in his mind, Samantha morphed into

Morgan and he saw himself sending his seed into his stepdaughter instead. This crazy thought sent him over the brink even more and it seemed that before he finished cumming one time he began anew and squirted more than he ever had.

When he finished, he felt ashamed of thinking of Morgan in the same way he thought of Samantha but at the same time the thought of cumming in that tight little hole with no protection was a turn-on that was starting to make him rise again.

Obviously, the shower was not doing the trick and since all he was accomplishing was a higher water bill, he conceded that he may as well get out and fight the feelings like a decent man would do. So that is what he decided he would do. For all intents and purposes, Morgan was his daughter and he vowed he would not act upon his feelings for her, ever.

~

THE HOURS between then and the night's activities seemed to pass very quickly for Sean. He made Morgan her favorite lunch -- macaroni and cheese -- and gave her a birthday present. When Morgan saw it, she squealed like the five-year-old she looked like eating macaroni and cheese.

"Daddy it's beautiful," she cried, tears running down her cheeks as she took the delicate bracelet out of its box. It was fully loaded with charms, two of which he pointed out.

The first was a small gold circle with an 18 in the center.

The second had a small pink heart-shaped jewel with the word "daughter" just above it.

She leaped into his arms and cuddled him tight, covering his face with kisses. One of the kisses found his lips and for a moment Sean found himself enjoying, a little too much, his daughter's soft lips on his and her beautiful body pressed to his in the tight embrace.

"I'll wear it for dinner tonight." She beamed as she stepped back.

"I bought some other things for you too, they're upstairs on your bed." He smiled.

She raced off upstairs, and that was all he heard from her until she came downstairs to go for her birthday meal.

∼

SEAN CALLED FOR HER, and was waiting in the hallway -- freshly showered, shaven and dressed in a three-piece suit.

When Morgan came downstairs, he was adjusting the sleeves of his suit with his back to the stairs, but he heard her stop about halfway down.

"Do I look okay, Daddy?" her voice asked nervously.

"I'm sure you look...." was all Sean managed as he turned around.

What he saw stopped anymore words from forming and damn near stopped his breathing too.

Morgan was gorgeous.

Her coal black hair was tied back in a perfect braid, and her makeup was flawless, drawing attention to her beautiful green eyes. She was wearing a beautiful silk evening gown -- ivory white -- with her new bracelet around her right wrist, matching earrings, and see-through two-inch high heels.

"Wow....." was all he could say, as she truly had achieved in making him mute.

Apparently his expression said everything, as she smiled bashfully.

She continued down until she stood right in front of him at the foot of the stairs; Sean then extended his arm to her as he led her to the front door. Once they stepped out onto the driveway, this time it was her jaw that dropped and she was rendered speechless.

"A limo?" she shrieked.

"Only the best for my baby." He smiled.

"Shall we?" he asked her.

She answered with only a smile.

∾

THE MEAL PASSED QUICKLY, and Morgan found herself smiling at Sean quite a bit. There had been a tense moment when the waitress had called them a cute couple -- which had confused her for a moment until she realized the woman thought they were dating.

Morgan had looked at her daddy, unsure how he would handle this, but he simply smiled at the waitress that he was a lucky man. Morgan beamed, and was secretly pleased, that he had not bothered to correct the waitress.

When it was over -- the last course being an absolute divine bowl of chocolate-covered strawberries and champagne -- they were driven back home -- by limousine again -- with Morgan clinging onto his arm and her head on his shoulder.

Once home, she knew the time had come to speak to her father about the real reason she had wanted a meal alone.

∾

"DADDY? Can we talk? I need to tell you something but I don't want you to be angry with me."

"I'll never be angry with you honey. Come and sit down," he answered, sitting on the sofa and patting the space beside him. Morgan sat down, but in the chair across from him.

"It's about mom -- sort of," she said quietly, and his face dropped for a second.

"Okay. Go ahead," he replied eventually.

"How come you haven't dated since mom died?" she asked.

Sean was caught off-guard and not sure how to answer, "I... There's never been anyone I've been interested in since then. And besides, I have you."

Morgan's breath caught in her throat, then he continued.

"I already have one special woman in my life – you -- so I don't need another to mess up the peaceful life we have together. That's not to say I have objections to you finding someone to settle down with."

Morgan broke down in tears. He immediately leapt off the sofa and wrapped his arms around her.

"What's wrong baby?" he asked, clearly worried. Morgan looked up at him, eye to eye.

"I love you, Daddy," she told him quietly.

"I love you too, baby." He smiled back, and Morgan knew he wasn't getting the message.

So she took his face in her hands and kissed him, soft and slow on the lips.

"I LOVE you, Daddy," she repeated in a feverish whisper, emphasizing the middle word with an intense look straight into his eyes that reached down into his soul as well as his pants when he finally caught the realization and true meaning of her words.

Sean leaned back, dumbfounded, unable to believe what his daughter had just said.

The look in her eyes was half panic, half relief, probably because she had wanted to say it for a while but was scared to in case he didn't feel the same way and it made things awkward between them.

Truthfully Sean felt the same way, but -- like her -- had

suspected she would be utterly horrified. In an attempt to tell her how he felt with actions rather than words, because he was sure words would fail him at the moment, he clasped his hands to the sides of her face and gently returned the same kiss she had just given him.

When he leaned back to see her reaction, she was smiling -- and it was the most beautiful sight he had ever seen.

"I love you too, Morgan," he told her.

He reached down and took her shoes off, slowly running his hand up her leg, over her lap and ending at her breast which he lightly rubbed through her dress making her breathe deeply and loudly as her body shivered beneath his touch. His eyes never left hers, nor hers his when he stood then, effortlessly and without another word, lifted her into his arms and carried her upstairs to his bedroom. Once there, he put her down next to the bed then kissed her again.

"Daddy?" she said in an innocent voice.

"Yes?"

"Make love to me," she requested.

Sean smiled, but only for a moment.

"Are you sure?" he asked, worried.

Morgan kissed him again.

"Yes Daddy, I'm sure." She nodded.

"Okay. First we have to get you undressed."

Sean noticed that Morgan was trembling so he kissed her again hoping it would quell her nerves. He assumed her apprehension was because of the fact that they were daddy and daughter and he certainly didn't want to ruin their current relationship so he said to her, "It's okay honey. We don't have to if you feel uncomfortable."

"It's not that Daddy, it's just... I've never..." she started, but lost the bravado and confidence she had felt just a few moments ago and fell quiet, looking away from him as her tears started to flow.

Her daddy seemed to know what she wanted to say, and took her face in his hands, making her look at him.

"Are you a virgin, honey?" he asked softly.

Morgan nodded, ashamed.

He turned her gently so that her back was to him. She presumed this was because he had decided this was not going to happen when she felt him tugging carefully at her hair. He untied her braid and when her hair tumbled free, he brushed it aside and kissed her neck and shoulders from behind. He then proceeded to unzip the gown, and she heard him gasp when he noticed what was underneath it.

She smiled boldly over her shoulder at him.

"I found you a present for my birthday too, Daddy." She giggled, referring to the set of exquisite underwear that had been purchased by her a few days before in hopes that this night would come. They were a bra and thong set, made of fine red lace with a white lace trim.

She heard him sit down heavily on the bed, and she turned to face him. He was staring up at her with an awestruck expression on his face, and her heart leapt.

"Do I look okay Daddy?"

"Incredible," he stammered.

Morgan started to unhook her bra, but he raised his hand to stop her. For a moment she thought he didn't want to see her naked, but he quickly removed all his clothing and after taking a moment to allow her a look at what she had in store for her, he slipped under the covers. Morgan smiled, then unhooked the bra and let it fall to the floor.

Then she slowly slid the thong down and let it fall on top of the bra she had just taken off.

The gleam in his eyes changed to sheer desire as he studied her naked body, making Morgan feel somewhat shy but at the same time overwhelmed with joy and arousal.

She was about to crawl into the bed next to him when

he stopped her again. "I want to see you touch yourself." Morgan raised her eyes to look directly into his and then without a word she placed one hand in her pussy and began rubbing rather harshly all around her clit down below while her other hand went to her tits and started pulling and yanking on her hard nipples going back and forth from one to the other. Just the fact that her daddy was watching made her hotter than usual so she was somewhat rougher with herself than she normally was when she was alone.

By asking her to put on a show for him, Sean was trying to hold off as much as he could because he was not sure if he could hold himself to soft and tender once he got his hands on her. He wanted her so badly and the display she was doing now only enriched the feelings. He couldn't hold back any longer. He raised the covers and she slipped into bed beside him, where he held her while trying to get control of his body and his need to plunder so he could take it slow knowing it was her first time. For several minutes, all they did was kiss. He rolled her onto her back, lying between her legs but not high enough for her to feel his erection. He kissed her neck, then trailed soft kisses down to her left breast where he gently clamped her very hard nipple between his lips.

Morgan moaned as pleasure raced through her young body. Then she moaned louder as he proceeded to softly twist and pull on her right nipple while he focused his oral attentions on her left one. He continued to lavish attention on both, going back and forth between the two, until the first non-masturbatory orgasm of her life exploded through her.

"DADDY!" she cried out as her body bucked wildly beneath him.

When the orgasm subsided, he kissed his way down her soft tummy, making her giggle momentarily as the kisses tickled her, then she moaned as a kiss landed on her inner thighs.

Then she felt it.

His tongue parted her virgin lips down below and delved deep inside. After a few moments of poking around inside, it retreated and circled her hard little nub, then slipped back inside again. Her daddy repeated this over and over, often breaking the pattern to suck firmly on her clit.

Morgan came again and again under her daddy's relentless attack on her most sensitive points. Eventually she pushed on his shoulders in a plea for mercy, and he leaned up to look at her. When she saw her juices glistening on his lips, she shuddered in pleasure.

"Ready, baby?" he asked. Morgan bit her lip, still a little hesitant and scared but wanting more at the same time.

Sean, sensing she was uneasy told her, "We can stop anytime you want to baby."

Morgan looked at him on top of her and said, "I want to. I want to be your special girl in all things. I love you, Daddy. I want us to be more than daddy and daughter."

He moved up and kissed her, then looking her intently in the eyes, his face only mere inches from her face he told her, "You turned eighteen today, so you are no longer a girl but if we do this you will be a woman. A real woman and there will be no going back. Are you sure this is what you want?"

"Yes. I know people will look down on us for being in love with each other, but my heart wants only you. I don't care about others. No one else has to know about us, and we can start fresh somewhere people don't know us."

This was exactly what Sean wanted to hear. "Okay then, I'm going to help you become a woman."

He smiled then leaned over toward the small table next to the bed opening the drawer and began fumbling around.

"No, Daddy," Morgan said

"Huh?" Sean stopped and looked at her.

"No condom. I want to feel you inside me. I want you to fill me with your sperm."

"Are you sure?"

"Yes, Daddy."

Sean seemed unsure for a moment to continue but then nodded as his erection sat waiting impatiently at her tight entrance. As it slipped inside she squealed in slight pain, then felt herself stretch as he pushed ever so slowly deeper. He soon encountered her hymen and paused.

"I can do it quick or slow, baby. They'll both hurt but quicker is easier."

"Do it quick." She nodded.

Though still a little worried how she would handle it, he nonetheless gave her what she asked for and thrust in deep with one quick shove, tearing her hymen and filling her completely. Morgan let out a cry of agony and dug her nails into his back, but he didn't move a muscle except to kiss her slowly. Soon the pain subsided, she regained her breath and he felt her muscles started to relax.

"I'm okay," she assured him.

Then, and only then, did he begin to pull out slowly, and the sudden emptiness made her gasp. The sensation increased until he was almost out, then he pushed back in, filling her so much she cried again but this time in ecstasy instead of pain. He carried on this pace, whispering in her ear the whole time how well she was doing.

Morgan felt a giant climax approaching, and judging by Sean's rapidly ragged breathing and faster stride, so was he. This made Morgan smile, and she urged him on by wrapping her legs tighter round his waist. Moments later, he peaked, emptying his seed into her.

Morgan felt him when he came. Her insides felt warm

and wet and the thought that this was her daddy made her cum harder than she ever had.

It lit her entire body up with pleasure, making her entire body shake and causing her to cry out with unadulterated euphoria.

Her daddy collapsed on her, and they both relaxed limply on the bed. After they had both caught their breath, he rolled off her and she laid with her head on his chest.

"Daddy?"

"Yes honey?"

"I love you."

"I love you too Morgan."

"I want to marry you, have your babies. I --"

"Morgan, stop," he told her, forcing her to pause. "I want those things too, but we have to take care of one important thing first."

"Really? What?" inquired Morgan looking at her daddy uncertainly.

Sean got off the bed and walked over to get a book on a table in the other room then came back and climbed in bed next to Morgan. She looked at him confused as he started to open the book.

"What is it Daddy?"

"Well, first you have to stop calling me Daddy if we're going to be together as a man and a woman."

Morgan smiled at this and replied, "Alright... Sean."

"Next, once we start doing this on a regular basis, without protection, sooner or later something's going to happen and everyone around here knows you're my daughter so we've got to find a new place to live," he said as he started flipping pages in the book which Morgan could now see was a book of maps from everywhere in the world.

"Daddy?" Morgan said.

"Yes honey?"

"I love you, now fuck me again then later we'll find a place to live... Sean."

She smiled a devilish smile at him and it was too good to pass up as the book slid to the floor and he rolled back on top of her to start another round.

THE END
Get Access to over 20 more FREE Erotica Downloads at Shameless Book Deals

SHAMELESS BOOK DEALS is a website that shamelessly brings you the very best erotica at the best prices from the best authors to your inbox every day. Sign up to our newsletter to get access to the daily deals and the Shameless Free Story Archive!

PUMPKIN - WILLSIN ROWE

When Steve comes home to find his sexy brat flouting his rules and flaunting her curves, he decides it's time to give this untouched beauty a hard lesson. And if it should end up giving him an heir, then that will just be perfect.

The smell of gasoline, grease and sweat coated my clothes and my skin as I drove home. It had been a hot day at the dealership, with fussy customers and puffed up junior salesmen. Nothing ticked me off more than a pretty boy half my age trying to throw his weight around, just 'cause he wore a tie. The smarter ones only ever tried it once with me.

As chief mechanic of Lyon Autos, my office—if you could call it that—was always noisy, and even in winter, got so hot it could suffocate a python. I loved the work, and I was damn good at it, but home was where I found peace.

In the last year or so, things had gotten tense and heated there as well. It started when my then-wife, Rosanna, suddenly had a mid-life crisis and ran off to find herself; leaving me to care for her daughter on my own. Something I did a pretty fucking good job of, too.

My stepdaughter, Payton, had barely turned eighteen when her mom left. What was worse, though, was Rosanna blamed her daughter for all her own troubles. *"I'm too young to have a grown daughter."* Those were the last words either of us heard her say.

As I turned off the main road into my own street, images of Payton flashed into my mind. As long as I was being brutally honest with myself, I had to admit the real truth. And that was that Payton, in all her soft-bodied glory, was the real reason my home was tense and hot. When she was near me, the place felt as cramped as an elevator.

When I married her mom, Payton had been a slender and pretty fifteen-year-old. In the few years since she'd arrived, nature had put in double overtime on her body. She was languid, luscious, and—the part that seemed to bother her mom the most—legal.

Yeah, the skinny, underage cheerleader was no more. In her place was a full-figured nineteen-year-old goddess; tall, beautiful and with a curvaceous body that made me hard every goddamn time I was around her. If anyone asked me to describe the perfect woman, I wouldn't need to. I'd just point toward my stepdaughter.

I slammed on the brakes, sending my truck into a short skid to avoid rear-ending Trent Crawford's Beemer, which had slowed right down to turn off the street.

Dammit. When Payton's long legs came into my head, I was blind to everything else around me. As I made the turn into my own driveway, my cock strained against his denim jail. All because I was seconds away from seeing my stepdaughter again. I'm a strong man, but that girl was my Achilles heel.

It wasn't just the pout of her pretty mouth, or the bounce of her long hair that had me under her spell. It wasn't even the sway of her big tits or her wide hips. It was her bold sensuality that had me jerking off each and every night with nothing in my mind but Payton.

I mean, it seemed effortless; as if she lived and breathed sex. Like she was designed and built just for that purpose alone. Hell, there was barely a night—or day—that went past where I didn't hear moans and squeals of pleasure coming from her bedroom. It was the most amazing torture listening to the rasp of her voice as she reached the brink of climax, and the moaning sigh as she tumbled over the edge. The fact she never closed her door all the way was beyond a tease. It verged on cruelty to animals. It sure turned me into a horny hound dog.

So far, I'd never seen any boys—or girls, for that matter—sneaking in or out of her room, so I had to assume she had some excellent toys, or a set of fingers sent straight from heaven. Either way, the image in my head was more than enough to get my pulse racing.

As I drove into the garage, it was as if my fantasies had come to life. I was greeted by the ball-squeezing sight of Payton, standing beside my work bench, a light sheen of sweat coating her perfect skin—and there was plenty of that skin on show.

Her long, thick-thighed legs drizzled like honey from torn denim cutoffs down to her bare feet. The creamy skin of her breasts seemed to struggle for freedom from the crop top she was barely wearing. It was impossible not to notice she was braless.

She was tinkering with a couple of my tools, running her long-fingered hands over them like a game show model. She was, in fact, breaking at least two of my rules. Always wear shoes in the workshop, for one. And don't mess with my tools. I couldn't believe she'd forgotten. Seeing her standing there, barely clothed, it was fucking hard to get angry at her, though.

Killing the engine, I studied her as she studied me. She gripped one of my spanners and squeezed it, a cheeky grin scampered across her mouth for a second. That's when I realized she knew exactly which rules she was breaking. The brazen little minx.

For a moment, it was a classic Mexican standoff, before I caved and got out.

"Hey, Pumpkin."

"Hi, Daddy."

"You really don't have to call me that. You're a grown woman now. I'm fine if you want to call me Steven. Or even Steve."

"I know. But my dad never gave me a pet name. Too busy working out his own stuff. So I love it when you call me Pumpkin. It's kind of our thing."

I started calling her by that name as a joke. She was already a teenager by then, so I just did it in fun. But she'd smiled so wide I just kept on calling her that, figuring she'd let me know when to stop. So far, she hadn't.

Payton cut through my memories, taking my hand in hers. "Plus it's fun to have a big, strong man I can call Daddy. Makes me feel...safe."

Yeah, maybe she felt safe, but I felt dangerous. Okay, so I might not get thrown in jail, but if I crossed the line here it could still cost me.

Payton put her free hand on the side of my neck. "You're so hot. Let me take care of that for you." She sauntered over to the spare fridge and bent down to pull out a beer. All that did was give me the perfect view of her perfect ass as it forced its way out of those tiny shorts. There was no doubt in my mind now what she was doing. I couldn't fault her effort, but her subtlety was for shit.

She opened the bottle and brought it straight to me, pressing her delectable tits together with her arms. If she vamped it up any harder the fabric would give way. "Here you go, Daddy."

As she handed me the cold beer, she had a tiny lopsided smile on her pouty lips. As if that wasn't enticing enough, she brushed her fingers across the back of my hand, her soft skin singing against the roughness of mine. The sight and feel of her sent rapid pulses of hunger into my belly and down the length of my cock.

"Thank you, Pumpkin."

Her cheeks reddened at the use of her nickname. If that had ever happened before, I'd never noticed it. It threw an extra layer of cuteness onto her lush beauty. I slugged a long mouthful of cold liquid to fill the moment.

If I started anything here, I would most definitely finish it. A girl as young and innocent as Payton might not be up to the challenge, no matter how grown up she thought she was.

Before I could let myself go and touch her—*really* touch her—I headed through to the living room and flopped onto the sofa. Payton followed right behind.

I slugged another mouthful and decided to tackle the moment head on. "So, what is this thing you're trying to make happen between us, Pumpkin?"

Her mom always had the moves but Payton was clearly a smart understudy. Plus she had more delectable flesh on her bones than her mother ever had. Flesh that rippled and rolled like the ocean as she glided across the floor to me.

Payton knelt in front of the sofa and put her hands on my knees, leaning forward enough that her tits hung halfway out the skimpy top.

"I'm not trying to *make* something here. Don't you think

we already have everything? We're so close. What we have goes way deeper than stupid *family* ever could."

Oh, she definitely had the moves. With just a couple of sentences she made her mom the enemy, and paired herself with me. I had to admit, the touch of her hands, and the fresh feminine scent of her body, were almost impossible to resist.

I'm no Einstein, but I'm smart enough. I work long hours and I know cars. My hands are rough, my head is hard, and I bleed blue collar because that's the life I love. Thankfully it didn't take a genius to understand what was happening here.

"So, tell me Pumpkin…you really think you're ready for this?"

"I'm ready for anything."

I out down my beer and slid my fingers into her hair, cradling the back of her head. She mewed like a kitten and leaned into my touch. With nothing more than a tiny bit of moaning and nuzzling, she had my cock hard and my blood pumping.

"Pumpkin, you're too young to be so sure of yourself."

She stared up at me, her beautiful brown eyes like pools of hot coffee. "I don't care. I just want you, Daddy. I always have." She kissed my wrist and ran her hands up my thighs. "I'll do anything."

Damn. She had her hands right at the tops of my thighs. My cock was trying to punch through the zipper on my jeans. Her eagerness had me picturing just how fucking perfect her sweet little slit would be, how tight she'd feel, how pretty she'd look—and especially how she'd taste.

"Okay, Pumpkin. Remember, you wanted this."

"Of course, Daddy. I can handle myself."

"Believe me, I know that. These walls are thin."

"And I left my door open every time. Hoping you'd *accidentally* walk in on me, naked, with my legs spread and my fingers inside myself—"

"Dammit."

"—and then you'd have to punish me for being a bad, bad girl." She licked her lips and stared deep into my eyes. "And that's what I am, Daddy. A bad girl. *Your* bad girl."

I snapped my hand into a tight fist, pulling her hair taut against her scalp. The action made her cry out, but my girl needed to know just what kind of beast she was teasing.

I held her gaze and smirked. "You're too young to be *that* bad."

She trembled against me, and a sweet little grin skipped across her lips. "Do you know that every time I cum, it's 'cause I'm thinking about you, Daddy?"

I'd known women twice her age who couldn't work a man this well. Even blushing, she oozed with confidence in her own body. Even when her voice trembled, it still had that sexy little dry rasp. The kind that made me think she desperately needed fluids.

Without warning, I pulled her mouth against mine and drove my tongue inside. She whimpered against me and I couldn't tell if it was fear, arousal or a fucking beautiful mix of the two. Payton clawed at my arm like a small creature, trapped in the jaws of a wolf. She'd learn soon enough what being a bad girl meant to me.

When I pulled away from her, she dragged in a long breath, as if she'd been drowning. Her voice, when she finally spoke, was so low I could barely hear her.

"Oh, Daddy...that was perfect."

Every tiny move she made seemed perfectly designed to call my cock to attention. Despite having my fist still in her hair, she could get her hips shimmying, and her tits jiggling.

"Please, Daddy. Let me show how good I am at being bad. It's just you and me and I want..." She licked her lips and smiled. "I want to give you everything. I'll make you my king."

"I don't want to be your king." I glided my thumb across her full lips, parting them so I could thrust inside. "But I'll be your daddy…Pumpkin."

Payton sucked at my thumb and moaned at my words, and I loosened my hold in her hair. She slid her mouth off my thumb and smiled up at me. "I've wanted you for so long. Since before I even understood what it meant. I just knew I needed to be around you. Any day I made you happy was automatically a great day."

"Take me out."

"Wh–what?"

"You want to make me happy? Take my cock out."

She closed her eyes as her jaw drooped a little. "You mean it, Daddy?"

"I do, Pumpkin."

There was a strong trembling in her hands as she reached for my jeans. She clumsily worked them open, her nerves clearly making the movements difficult. As she drew them down, my cock sprang free, and she jumped in surprise.

"Ohh…" She stared hard at it like she'd never seen one up close.

"Pumpkin? You okay?"

She stared a moment longer then glanced up at me. "I–I'm sorry, Daddy. It's just, I didn't really think you'd let me and…and it's so big." She closed her eyes and a fresh burst of pink flushed her cheeks. "I've never actually been with anyone before."

I wasn't exactly surprised to find out she was a virgin. Though it did make me wonder how hard I could push her.

"Put your mouth on me, Pumpkin."

"What if I get it wrong?"

"You say you're a bad girl. Well, bad girls have to learn to do as they're told. Put my cock in your mouth."

Her breath pumped against the underbelly of my hard

beast as she wrapped her hands around my shaft. She shot one last glance up at me and then slid the thick head into her mouth.

Slowly, Payton eased more of my cock inside herself, the sweet humming of her voice vibrating against me. She seemed a little awkward, but really keen to learn. And who was I to deny a beautiful young woman the chance of an education?

"Pumpkin...take off your shorts."

She sat up, letting me slip out of her mouth.

"No, sweetie. Don't stop."

Payton seemed confused for a second, then bent back to her task of pleasing me. As she took half my cock into her mouth she slid her hands down to the front of her shorts. The shimmy of her hips as she worked the button and zip open was a thing of beauty.

She ground her tongue against my cock and tightened her lips around it as she pushed her shorts past her delicious wide hips.

"Slowly, Pumpkin. Make a show of it."

She moaned at first before letting me slip out again, long enough to answer, "Y-yes, Daddy." Barely had the words left her lips than she'd taken my length back inside.

Slowly, she rotated those rich hips and inched the worn denim lower and lower, taking her panties down for the ride. Once she had them to her ankles, I lifted her mouth off me.

"Stand up, Pumpkin."

She did as I told her, easing her feet out of the tiny shorts, and giving me the perfect view of her juicy little cunt. Bare in every way.

I stood and signaled her to step closer. The moment she did I seized her flimsy top and tore it from her body. Her squeal of surprise was almost as beautiful as the shimmy of her full breasts.

The force of my hand overbalanced her and she fell against the sofa. I seized her hips and pushed, pressing her face down into the leather as I knelt behind her. Before she could speak, I planted my mouth against the sweet, fragrant heart of her young pussy.

The full glory of her scent hit me, and she washed against my tongue. The wet heat of her seared my lips as I devoured her.

"Oh, Daddy…that's so good…" she moaned into the sofa.

I stopped licking her long enough to wet my fingers. As I tightened my teeth around her clit, I glided the tip of one finger inside her.

Her glistening slit tightened around me, and all I could think was how fucking amazing it would feel when I had my cock in there.

I pushed a finger up against the tight, puckered ring of her ass hole. Payton gasped as I eased the first joint inside her, and her knees trembled like crazy. "Daddy, what are you doing to me?"

I got my feet under me while still crouching and slowly ran my tongue up the sticky treat of her cunt, over her cheeky little ass hole and up the length of her back. "Exactly what you think you want. *Everything.*"

"Ohh…"

"You know what they say, sweet girl…be careful what you wish for."

"You know what I wish for." She swallowed, and her voice came out even softer, and higher. Like she was a little girl again. "You. Your mouth, your cock, your wonderful strong body."

I surprised her by scooping her up into my arms and carrying her down the hall. "You deserve the full treatment, Pumpkin."

Payton's soft but solid weight in my arms was a sweet

pleasure. The older I got, the more I knew myself, and my own desires. And there was nothing that filled me with want more than a plump, pear-shaped goddess. God, I could sink myself into every damn inch of this girl. All of me against all of her. Skin on skin, mouth on pussy, bone-to-bone. It would be the kind of heaven I'd gladly pay for. And if my Pumpkin was as good at fucking as she was at teasing, then this was going to be a night of ecstasy.

"Where are you taking me, Daddy?"

"To the bedroom, of course."

"Oh..." She rolled and squirmed until she could rest her head on my shoulder. "At last."

"You best remember you wanted this, little girl."

"It's all I've ever wanted."

Placing her on the bed face down, I slipped off my grimy work clothes and climbed on above her, one knee either side of her perfect ass. I reached for her shoulders and ran my hands down the length of her arms, pulling her wrists together at the small of her back.

With her arms held securely in my fist, I ran my other hand softly over the silken skin of her ass, and she let a tiny sigh stumble out of her throat. It was smooth at first, but when it cracked and turned dry it kicked me in the balls. There wasn't a single thing this girl did or said that didn't make me hard as a fucking rail.

"Holy fuck, Pumpkin."

A tremble ran through her curvaceous body. "Daddy, do you know how much I love it when you call me that?"

The sound of my palm landing on her ass was like a rifle shot, or a drum beat. It sure was music to my ears.

"Wh-what are you doing now?"

"Marking my territory."

"Ohh..."

Every swat of my hand filled my belly with want, and my

cock with need. The shimmy and shake of her gorgeous young flesh was hypnotic. And with every smack her skin further ignited with a red glow.

Every couple of slaps, I stopped and rubbed the tortured area, and Payton took deep breaths that stumbled in and stuttered out. "Wh-why does that feel so fucking good?"

"You said it yourself; you've been a bad girl, Pumpkin. Bad girls need consequences. And this is only the start."

I slipped my hand between her luxurious thighs and she stiffened for a second before she let her body liquefy. Her soft voice came out in a moan as I found the inferno of her sweet young cunt with my fingertips. I made a small circling motion and it was like I'd turned on a faucet. She coated my skin with her juices, and filled my ears with her tiny sobs of pleasure. When the heady scent of her pussy hit my nose full force it drove spears of lust through me.

"Pumpkin, do you trust your daddy?"

"Uhh... *yesss...*"

"Good girl."

Her obedience was as erotic as her body. I rewarded her with a quick stab of my finger against her clit, knowing the sensation would be a sweet and painful overload of pleasure. Her surprised squeal worked its magic on me.

Drawing my fingers up to my nose, I savored the spicy oceanic scent of Payton. "Sweet Jesus, Pumpkin. You're perfect."

"Let me taste?"

I slid my wet fingers up the length of her body and she turned her face. With a little sigh, she latched on and sucked her own juices from my skin as she rolled onto her back.

"Thank you, Daddy," she whispered, then pulled my fingers back into her pretty mouth.

"Spread those long legs for me."

She did exactly as I told her, without any question.

Thanks to the dance lessons I'd funded for years, she was sweet grace and feminine power. I caressed her beautiful face with my scented fingers.

A long, low growl filled the room and it took me a moment before I realized it was coming from deep inside me. My cock was roaring at me, pulsing with need to be inside this girl. Anywhere and everywhere she could fit me.

When Payton pulled her mouth off my fingers, she made a dirty sweet smacking sound, then licked them like they were little cocks. She looked up at me with those big brown eyes of hers and shot me in the heart with a lop-sided grin.

"Mmm...I love how I taste."

I slid my hand down to her throat and gently caressed the skin there. She sighed and closed her eyes, and for a moment I considered going easy on the kid.

A tornado of conflicting emotions and needs spun through me. Anger and desire swirled against each other and there was no clear winner. Sure, I could go easy on Payton. Take her softly and gently, and spoon with her afterward.

But fuck that noise. She wanted to believe she was a big girl, so she was going to learn just what that meant.

I'm a big guy, and that intimidates a lot of women. I'd never had a lover before who wanted—maybe even needed—the kind of heavy-handed, physical fucking that came naturally to me. The kind where you pour your soul into the other person.

Truth be told, Payton wasn't ready for that, either. I was about to be her lover, but those step-fatherly instincts were still strong. What mattered now was to bring her pleasure. The pleasure of pain could wait.

From what I'd seen, though, she had it in her to become everything I needed. With time and training.

My girl closed her eyes as I leaned down and kissed her. Just a soft touch of lips on lips this time, and she sighed into it. The scent of her pussy called to me, though, and I drifted quickly down to quench my thirst.

Drinking her juice was like alcohol mixed with freefall. The taste and scent of her pussy made me light-headed and heavy-handed.

"Oh... Daddy..."

She must have known how much that name affected me. Hearing it trickle from her sweet mouth as I drank from her even sweeter slit was sheer perfection. And while it made my body hard as steel, it turned my head to mush.

I ran the face of my tongue over her beautiful hair-free pussy, exploring every inch, every millimeter, every pore of her. Pressing with the tip and scouring with the rough top, searching for every way she could possibly taste. Her sighs and squeals were better than any music.

Payton put her hands on my head and pulled her knees up, drawing her body open to me and begging without words for me to go harder, faster. As she rested her feet on my shoulders I slapped my palms onto her most tender skin, either side of my fleshy wet feast.

I dragged outward, pulling her lips wide apart and driving my tongue deep inside her. The flavor was even more intense, and it got my insides howling harder than they already had been. I pulled her juicy fat lips into my mouth and sucked on them, hard enough to make her draw breath.

"Oh, Daddy... you're so..."

Already she was struggling to talk, but Payton was going to be breathless and mute by the time I finished her off. I had no doubt she'd cum like crazy on the end of my cock, but my job would only feel half done if I didn't bring her off with the heat of my mouth first.

As I ran my tongue up to her clit she whimpered, and when I took that tiny bud between my teeth she tensed up. The heat, the juice, the scent of her were a symphony. She was fresh and ready, and if I lost my head for even a second I'd give everything up just to satisfy my own needs. To bury myself in this young woman. To let her essence swamp me... drown me. I'd be getting there soon enough. But first there was the little matter of her climax.

When I squeezed my teeth around her hard little clit, she gasped and tightened her grip on my hair, pulling all my body's sensations up to my scalp. Pain and pleasure rolled into one beast, igniting like a brush fire in my head and then spilling slowly down the length of my back. The desire was a wild creature riding me, sinking its claws into my belly as I sank my teeth into her cunt.

I surprised her by pulling my mouth off her for a second. Only long enough to reach up and grasp one of her big boobs and squeeze. Payton looked down at me, confusion and arousal written on her face. Biting into her clit again got me the exact response I was looking for, and she bucked her hips off the bed. I slid my tongue down, right down, past the end of her sweet cunt and into the dark depths of her ass crack. The rippled flesh of her tender young hole glanced over the wet tip of my tongue and she widened her eyes as if she'd seen a ghost.

"Daddy, you shouldn't...ohhh..."

It took every bit of my willpower to pull my mouth away long enough to answer. "And who's going to stop me?"

Before she spoke again I pinched her nipple and made a tiny circling movement with my tongue.

"Mmm...not me."

"Good girl, Pumpkin."

God, she made me hot when she writhed beneath me. I wanted to sink my teeth into every curvy fucking inch of her. I lashed at her with my tongue, soaking her already wet pussy as I came back up to suck on her cheeky little clit.

I drank a little more from the sweetness of her pussy and

then pulled free again, hooking my hand under her leg and flipping her over onto her belly.

"Daddy, what are you doing?"

"Shh, Pumpkin. Daddy's eating."

I bit into the firm but soft flesh of her nineteen-year-old ass and the squeal she let loose made my cock jump like he'd been Tasered. I seized her hips and pulled on her until that big beautiful ass was propped up at the edge of the bed, ready for whatever I did to it.

"You're fucking perfect, Pumpkin."

"Daddy..."

Still kneeling, I drove my tongue deep inside her pussy as I gripped the soft, full cheeks of her ass. Lapping at her heat, sucking on her flesh, I couldn't stop myself moaning and growling like a beast. Yeah, I had the power here...but fuck me, it was almost impossible to hold back.

With my tongue circling her clit I pulled her sweet peach apart, opening up that immaculate candy-pink hole. The beast within me roared, demanding I get my cock inside her as soon as possible.

As big as I am, though, and with her being a virgin, I knew I'd have to ease my way in.

So instead of my cock, I glided my finger into her, twisting my hand as I pushed, stretching her out and forcing fresh squeals from deep within her.

When Payton found her voice again it had the softness of a kitten. "Daddy...Daddy..."

The driving of my finger drew out a fresh burst of her fucking incredible scent. It took everything I had not to put my mouth back on her. Payton was an absolute treat for the senses.

And a goddamn tease, too. She lowered her chest to the bed and held her pretty ass high, as if begging me to use my other hand to spank her.

"You really don't know what's good for you, do you, Pumpkin?"

"Oh, yes I do." She turned her head and looked me in the eye. "You, Daddy."

I pushed a second finger inside her and a ripple flowed through her sweet body. Her voice cracked and became nothing more than a rasp. I rolled my hand as I pumped in and out, the knuckles of my fingers finding new places to touch her with every drive. When I had my fingers all the way inside her I hooked them, pressing down onto that sweet spot at the front. As I ground her clit with my thumb I gave in and licked the gorgeous cheek of her ass.

"Oh, my God…"

"Right now, Pumpkin, that's exactly what I am."

"Y-yes, Daddy."

"And you, sweet girl, are going to cum. It's going to be big, and it's going to be soon. Then—and only then—will I let you have my cock."

"Oh…Daddy…spank me again?"

The desire in her voice cut away the last of my control. It was only my own need to see her cum—to really see it—that got me through. "Soon, Pumpkin."

I licked the thumb of my free hand and glided it down onto her tight, puckered ring. Payton gripped the sheets a little tighter as the corner of her pretty mouth curled up. Slowly, with just a little pressure, I made circles on her rippled flesh with the hard knuckle. My girl sighed so sweetly I couldn't help smiling myself.

Still gliding my fingers in and out of her pussy, I bent my thumb until the tip of it was kissing her ass hole. I pressed, and she squirmed, but didn't flinch. Her tiny smile turned harder as she frowned, and a sweet little groan fell from her throat. God damn it, she was perfection.

When I had the full tip of my thumb inside her, I kissed the fleshy cheek of her ass. "Are you ready, Pumpkin?"

"Yes, Daddy. Ready for anything."

"Then let go. Cum when you feel it."

As soon as I finished speaking, I sank my teeth into her soft flesh. With one thumb in her ass, one on her clit, and two fingers teasing inside her, that last touch of pain seemed to finish the job. Payton pulled at the sheets, lifting her head and dragging in breath after deep, sucking breath. She bucked against me, her cunt tightening so hard she nearly crushed my fingers.

For just a moment she grew still, then as if falling from a tree, she rolled her hips, arched her back and squealed as a climax punched through her beautiful curvy body.

Before the pulsations had even finished, I stood and pulled my fingers from inside her. Payton was at the perfect height, and her glistening pussy beckoned. I stepped forward and nudged the fat head of my cock up to her entrance.

"Ohh..." Her voice was deep and smoky, like she'd suddenly taken the final step to womanhood. The sexy sound of it made me shudder with an even greater want.

It filled me with strength and even gave me hope. Hope for a future I hadn't been considering. With a beautiful woman by my side and a family to care for.

Holy fuck. I'd never thought that way before. Not with Rosanna, and certainly not before her. But Payton's already curvy body had awoken something inside me. In a flash, I pictured her round belly swollen with child, her full breasts even fuller...and holy fuck it turned me on.

"Pumpkin, I'm going to drive you fucking wild."

"You have been for fucking years, Daddy."

Those words took my last shred of restraint, and I inched my hips forward, gliding my thickness into her pussy and bellowing at the heavens.

"Daddy," she said, her voice trembling. "Y-you're so big."

"I warned you to be careful what you wish for. I'm taking you now, at my speed and bare. You're going to feel every inch of me."

"Oh, my..."

Of course, I wasn't just going to plow into her like a savage. But she'd talked a big game earlier. A little reality check wouldn't do her any harm.

Slowly, I rocked forward and back, as her tight little snatch opened for me. As much as I needed to be buried in her up to the hilt, I'd already promised myself not to be a self-serving prick here. Besides, I wasn't about to hurt the woman who was hopefully going to become the mother of my child.

It had only been a moment since I'd thought about it, but already that desire had grown. The need to fill her. Not just with my cock, but with my seed.

It took over a minute—which felt like a century—before I was completely inside her, but fuck it was worth the wait. The inferno of her, all over the skin of my cock, was the sweetest pain I'd ever known.

She squeezed me like an angry fist and I never wanted to leave. The heat of her passion and the fire of her body called to me.

I grasped those beautiful wide hips and squeezed, her soft flesh spilling through my fingers almost like cream. It took a huge effort to pull myself out. The warm air felt cold as it bit into the wet skin of my shaft.

"Pumpkin... you're fucking amazing."

I drove back into her and she squealed. Her perfect skin had a gorgeous sheen of moisture, and knowing I'd caused it was amazing.

As I drove in and out of her sweetness, I ran my fingers over the skin of her back, gliding across the flawless surface as I explored her. She was velvet and satin, she was springy yet firm, and she whimpered at every touch of my rough hands.

Her voice sounded sticky in her throat as she spoke. "Fuck me, Daddy. Fuck me good..."

The little minx nearly sank me with those words. It was time to remind her who was boss here, so I took her long hair in my fist and tightened up. She screamed as I pulled and it made my cock jump inside her. I knew my own strengths; it would be my biggest pleasure learning Payton's.

"Pumpkin?"

"Yes, Daddy?"

"You're my good girl."

She tightened around me in a sharp clutch and it took my breath away. A few more seconds of that and I'd be over the edge.

With one mighty drive I slammed my hips against her ass, releasing her hair at the same time. Payton fell forward, gliding off my cock, and I swooped on her, rolling her over onto her back. Every delectable curvy inch of her shimmied, from her big perfect tits, through her rounded belly and down to her thick, juicy thighs.

I dived onto the perfection of her body, suckling at her hard nipples as I drove my hips forward. Searching blindly with my cock for the splendor of her magnificent cunt, I licked and sucked at her tits, her shoulder, her satin-soft throat. A moment later I was right there, at the entrance to home. With one fierce pump I pounded my hips forward, filling her again with my hardness.

The luxurious softness of her body beneath me was heaven, and I speared my fingers up into her hair. As I ground my cock into her body, I held her head still, keeping eye contact with her as we fucked.

"I am going to fill you, sweet Pumpkin."

"Oh...you are, Daddy."

"You're gonna be even sexier carrying our baby."

"Wh-what?" Her pretty eyes widened. "You want to...you want *me* to...?"

"You're already perfect. It'll be the cherry on top."

"Daddy..." Even through her obvious fear, she still gasped with pleasure, and moaned at my every thrust. "I don't know if I...if I can..."

I ground my hips against hers, holding myself fully inside her as I kissed her perfect mouth. "Oh, you can, sweetie. It's what I want more than anything. So you'll do it just for me."

A short burst of tears rolled down her cheeks as she smiled. "You're the only man I could ever trust, Daddy." She put her palm to my cheek. "Fill me."

When Payton hooked her fingers around my neck and pulled, I really let myself go. She scratched her nails into my skin and dragged me down into a kiss that came from the dark ages. She suckled on my tongue like it was food while I plundered her with my cock. Her sweet juices were still all over my face, and she simply lapped at my cheeks, and bit my lips. The little whimpering moans she made drove me even wilder. I bucked at her, throwing jabs and uppercuts with my hips, and I knew I was only moments away from cumming like a force of nature.

Payton pulled her mouth off me and sucked a sharp breath in through clenched teeth. "Oh, Daddy... I'm..." Her short barking squeals were the only other sounds that came from her as another climax ripped through her voluptuous body. That was everything I'd needed, and the fire in my belly turned supernova.

"Ah!"

"Daddy? Cum inside me. Make me whole."

I was already too far gone to stop, even if I wanted to. I

thundered against her and her perfect body rolled with every punch of my hips.

A moment later I was gone. I fisted her hair and shuddered, losing sight of her as I howled at the moon, driving my cock home as I pumped jet after jet of hot fluid into her.

Payton moaned and hissed. I shuddered with the final throes of orgasm and released her hair.

When I came to rest, Payton slid herself out from under me. She bent down and sucked hard on my shaft, cleaning her own scent off my skin and pulling out the last of the juice from deep inside me. When she popped her mouth off the end, she lapped me all over like a cat drinking cream.

I was still hard, and the way she smiled up at me while she squeezed my cock, I wasn't sure she'd ever let me go soft again. She was more than just temptation...she was a goddess.

"We taste perfect together, Daddy."

I brushed her now-messy hair back off her forehead and cupped her cheek. I'd never expected a girl so young and inexperienced could match me, blow for blow, and still come out smiling.

"Pumpkin, you deserve the best."

She gave me one long, sweet lick, from balls to tip, then kissed my cock on the nose. "And now, I have you."

I pressed her down onto her back and put my hand on her sweet belly. "And who knows? Maybe more."

She put both her hands over the top. "You're already everything, Daddy. But if we don't score this time, then we'll just have to keep on trying. Every day."

"You *are* a bad girl."

"I do my best."

THE END

Get Access to over 20 more FREE Erotica Downloads at Shameless Book Deals

SHAMELESS BOOK DEALS is a website that shamelessly brings you the very best erotica at the best prices from the best authors to your inbox every day. Sign up to our newsletter to get access to the daily deals and the Shameless Free Story Archive!

RAVISHING RHONDA - LENORE LOVE

Rhonda and the man of the house attend a friend's wedding together. She asked him to be her date because she thought he would be safe.

But while they dance to a slow sexy tune at the reception, something hard and hot looms between them, tempting Rhonda's innocence with urges that are shockingly impure. She knows these emotions are also dangerously taboo, but as he sensually sways against her nubile body, her resolve begins to weaken.

The thought of this big strong man being the first is too exciting to deny, and once back in the darkened confines of their suite, Rhonda becomes enslaved to her forbidden desires -- rough, raw, and unprotected!

𝒯he hotel ballroom was noisy and hot.

I sat alone at our table, watching couples gyrate vigorously on the dancefloor. The band was a little out of tune, and the music was way too retro for my taste. But Jenny was the bride, and she always leaned toward disco while we were growing up. Me, I was a blues fan like my father.

Jenny had wanted me to be in the wedding itself, but my schedule wouldn't allow it. To tell the truth, I was secretly relieved. But I hadn't wanted to come alone, and so I'd asked my father. I knew I'd be safe from unwanted advances with him around.

From the get-go, however, Dad had encouraged me to mingle, so I *had* danced with one of the groomsmen. He was okay at first, but when he groped my backside during a slow one, I left him standing there with a stupid look on his face. There was no point in allowing him to go further -- I had no intention of relinquishing my virginity to a guy I'd just met.

I gazed around the room, searching for my father but not seeing him. That was unusual because he was a man who stood out in a crowd. Tall, solidly built, with the brightest blue eyes you'd ever want to see and a humor that was infectious. At *soirées* like this, the women gravitated to him like moths to white light. But my mother had been the sole light of his life, and since she'd left, he had eyes for no other.

I left my seat and made my way through the crowd, wondering if he'd gone back to our suite. I passed through some French doors and stepped out onto the veranda; it was cooler out here, and I breathed deeply of the freshness. My dress was tight -- cut high on the thigh and low in front -- and I tugged at it, sighing with relief as that coolness flowed into my cleavage.

As I glanced around, I saw my father standing alone at the

veranda railing, his back to me. He was a mere silhouette in the darkness, hovering just beyond the amber light spilling through the ballroom's windows. I watched a small orange coal move from his mouth to the railing, and realized he was smoking a cigarette. I should have been surprised, but strangely, I wasn't.

"Hey, you," I said, walking over.

He turned, smiling faintly. "Hey, gorgeous."

I stood beside him, gazing out over the railing at the crescent moon riding the horizon, and returned his smile.

"I wondered where you went."

"Sorry. I didn't mean to sneak off."

Yes, you did, I thought. "What're you doing out here by yourself?"

He sighed heavily. "I don't know... Thinking, I guess."

I knew what he was thinking about, so I didn't bother to ask.

"You're supposed to be keeping me company, you know," I chided him softly. "We haven't danced or anything."

"Sorry about that, too."

He slipped his arm around me, and I snuggled against him, feeling his warmth and the security it provided. We were silent for a moment, and then I cleared my throat.

"So, when did you start smoking again?"

He sighed again. "When you were at school. The divorce has been rough."

I'd been four when he and my mother had married, and he'd adopted me a year later at her request. She'd wanted all of us to have the same last name -- be a real family. But she'd turned forty last year, and suddenly had to *discover* herself. I'd always heard about mid-life crises, but I'd never considered it could happen to my mother -- she'd always been so confident and sensible. I hadn't spoken with her since she'd left, and the intense sympathy I now felt for the only father I'd ever known made me shiver.

"I'm so sorry, Daddy."

"It's not your fault."

"I know that. But smoking's not going to help."

His faint smile looked genuine enough, but those baby-blues were sad. I watched him blow a lazy gray cloud into the night sky. It swirled for a moment and then vanished.

"You sound like your mother," he said quietly.

"Don't compare me to her," I replied quickly, and more sharply than I had intended.

He looked at me strangely for a moment, and then pursed his lips in disapproval.

"Now, you *really* do."

"I'm sorry, Daddy," I replied quickly. "I didn't mean to give you a hard time."

"It's not that. I'm just feeling a little drained."

I touched his arm. The peculiar way he looked at my slender fingers resting on his flesh made the hair on my neck stand up.

Oh Daddy, I thought, and my heart went out to him.

The band started a slow blues tune, and we both turned our heads toward the ballroom. The emotion evoked was raw and smoky and sensuous, and I suddenly felt the same. I smiled an invitation and held out my hands.

He hesitated for a second, and then finally nodded, wrapping his arms around my shoulders and pulling me close. For the first time in my life, I didn't feel my father. I just felt a man, lost and lonely and maybe even a little afraid. My mouth went dry and my heart surged.

"I just love this song," he murmured. "It reminds me of the old days."

I wasn't sure to which old days he was referring -- those times before Mom, or during. All I knew at that moment was that he needed my comfort and reassurance, and I intended to be there for him.

I slipped my arms around his waist, and pressed him closer still. My breasts flattened comfortably against his chest, and his pelvis moved sensually upon mine. The muscles in his back were lean and firm beneath my fingertips, and I smelled his cologne and the cigarette smoke that clung to his clothes. For some reason, I thought the odor was completely masculine, and a tiny chill shivered in my tummy.

"Daddy," I whispered. "Everything will be okay."

We swayed slowly to the music, our bodies moving as one. It felt so soothing to be held this way, and I enfolded myself further into his strength. I sighed contentedly, my heart beating steadily.

"Thanks for being here, Daddy."

"My pleasure, baby girl."

The song's sensual rhythms continued. I murmured something under my breath, lost in my father's comforting arms. Our soft gentle friction awakened my nipples in my pads, and I felt an erotic tingling prickling lazily through my chest. I wondered if he could feel them, and found it didn't matter. I caressed his back, humming along with the tune.

My father moaned softly, and my senses abruptly swam in amazement. He had grown erect, his penis literally bulging inside his trousers. It seemed incredibly long and abundantly thick, its steamy insistence pressing against my mound. When I finally came to grips with the fact that I was turning him on, something totally indecent dampened my untried portal, consuming me with shameful excitement. My hard nipples swelled more painfully than before, and my heart thundered against my ribs.

"You're shivering, Gwendolyn," he whispered, his breath warm on my cheek. "Aren't you enjoying the dance?"

Gwendolyn was my mother's name.

I gasped reflexively, trembling with arousal and embarrassment, and unable to reply. Did he not realize what he had just said, and what it might imply? Did he not know that I could *feel* his smoldering hardness, every throbbing muscular inch? Dazedly, I wondered if he was wearing any briefs -- it definitely didn't feel like it. I was only eighteen; I'd never experienced anything this intimate with a boy, let alone a man like my father, and I had no idea what to do.

He held me tighter. Helplessly, I rested my head upon his shoulder and shuddered. My dress was backless; I felt him tenderly caressing my shoulder blades, and then moving slowly down my spine. I nearly swooned when he cupped my bottom and squeezed, lifting me up on my toes and grinding his erection against my slit. Even that silly groomsman hadn't tried this.

My heart pounded and my breathing turned hoarse. Sudden pleasure wrenched my loins, unbidden and distressing -- warm wetness soaked my panties, slicking the insides of my thighs and clinging to my sodden pubic curls. I gasped, my corpulent folds pulsing as urgently as his organ, while my muddled emotions collided like meteors.

"Oh God, Daddy," I croaked.

"Gwendolyn," he breathed. "I love you so much."

He tilted my head back and kissed me. It was not an innocent father-daughter kiss. It was the kind of kiss a man delivers to a woman, firm and insistent. His lips explored mine hungrily, followed by the tip of his tongue. I tasted his cigarette, and wedding champagne. I moaned deep in the back of my throat, lost in desire that was dangerously forbidden.

Thankfully, the song ended and we broke apart. My father was breathing hard, and his gleaming blue eyes regarded me expectantly in the darkness, perhaps wondering if I were wet down below, and maybe even smelling it. My mouth moved soundlessly as I studied his bulging turpitude -- moisture darkened a coin-sized area where his turgid knob had seeped.

All at once, as if a plug had been pulled, the intensity fled his eyes and was replaced by a shameful sorrow that nearly brought me to tears.

"Oh my God, baby," he rasped. *"I'm so fucking sorry..."*

He turned and fled the veranda, disappearing into the hotel. I stood there stupidly, still tasting his tongue in my mouth.

～

HOURS LATER, I snuck like a thief into the black confines of my room, my heart pounding with adrenaline. I stared at the door that adjoined my father's room to mine, wondering if he was asleep. I hoped so; I couldn't face him just yet -- the scene on the veranda remained a stark, immoral memory. I had experienced all the confusion and guilt you would expect, but also a frightening desire that went far beyond family bonds, and maybe that's what I felt guilty about the most.

I suddenly felt very dirty. I peeled off my dress and panties, and then went into the bathroom. I turned on the shower, and became enslaved to my prurient arousal.

I imagined kissing my father again and running my fingers through his hair, while his hard naked shaft pushed insistently against my puling slit, demanding that I grasp and guide it. I moaned, envisioning its wall-stretching girth sliding between my wet runneled v-lips, punching through my maidenhead and filling me to the brim.

Shuddering, I squirted soap into my hands and massaged my nipples. They burgeoned like thimbles, demanding to be tongued; I closed my eyes rapturously and pinched them, groaning with bliss. I slid my hands down my soft round tummy, firmly cupped my hairy mound, and gently stroked my stiff, gristly clit. A perverse jolt of ecstasy wracked my shivering body, and I barely stifled a cry.

My head whirled and my thighs quivered as I thumbed my nub and plunged two fingers in and out of my tight virgin cooze. I gasped for breath, humping my groin wantonly, a Mack truck rolling steadily toward me. My father slept only a few feet away as I brazenly relived our gross encounter. The salacious intensity of my filthy desire was overwhelming -- and so utterly, monstrously wrong.

An orgasm rocked me powerfully, clenching my butt cheeks and curling my toes with joint-popping strength. I bit my lower lip, my ratcheting grunt echoing off the tiled walls as juice squirted across my busy fingers and joined the hot water streaming down my thighs.

I pictured my father between my legs, his strong hands grasping my bottom and locking my squirming pelvis to his, while he drove his rigid manhood deeply and repeatedly inside me, his mouth open and his bright blue eyes staring down at me. Another pulsing ejaculation ripped me in half, and this time I did wail, uncontrollably and libidinously -- my legs gave way and I crumpled onto the shower floor.

I had no idea how long I lay there like that, but when I finally regained my senses, the entire bathroom had filled with steam. My mind felt blank and my body was drained. I'd never experienced multiples like this, and their ferocity had been shamefully exhilarating.

Dazed, I turned off the water and stepped out onto the tile. My heart pounded like a four-alarm bell, and my breathing was shaky and uneven. I grabbed a towel off the rung and walked into the bedroom, trembling as I dried myself. I bent over and tossed my hair, toweling it dry. When I stood up, I locked eyes with my father.

He stood in the doorway that separated our suite, dressed for bed in loose boxers, his face filled with concern. He didn't seem embarrassed by my nudity, but I surely was.

"Daddy, I'm naked!"

I draped the towel in front of me as best I could. Being hotel linen, it sure didn't cover much. He offered me a small shrug, but didn't reply. I looked longingly at my dress rumpled on the bed, and cleared my throat.

"What're you doing in here?"

He shuffled his feet. "I heard you cry out. Are you okay?"

I blushed. I had no idea how much noise I'd actually made, let alone how much he might have heard.

"I'm okay, Dad."

He nodded, almost to himself, and turned to leave. My chest heaved, and I blurted out, "Daddy, wait."

He paused, but didn't turn around. "Yes?"

I wanted to ask if he'd thought about what happened between us, and if he felt anything -- any remorse or disgust or excitement. I wanted to know if he was angry with me or if he thought I was angry with him. I was desperate to know so many things, but all I said was, "You called me Gwendolyn."

My father turned around, his expression curious.

"I did?" He paused. "I don't remember that."

And then, he appeared to slip away like he had on the veranda.

"Your mother cried out when she climaxed," he said quietly. "You sounded just like her."

My blush deepened. "Daddy, that's gross."

But my heart began to pound, and my slit tingled traitorously. I watched him absently squeeze the front of his boxers, a weird look on his stubbled face.

"Is that what you were doing?" he asked, moving into the room. "Climaxing?"

Suddenly, he looked like a jungle animal stalking its prey. His blue eyes gleamed intently, and his teeth were exposed between his lips. I'd never seen him this way before, and I was suddenly both deeply frightened and helplessly thrilled.

"Well, were you?" he demanded.

I nodded wordlessly, my mouth growing dry. He nodded again.

"Were you thinking of me?"

I didn't know what to say, my fear and excitement overloading my reason. He now stood so close I could feel the heat of his body through the towel that separated us.

"Answer me, young lady," he snapped.

My body broke out into goosebumps in response to his authoritative tone. I'd rarely heard it as a child, but it always required strict obedience when I did.

"Yes, Daddy," I breathed. "I was thinking of you."

The words hung between us for a few silent seconds, and then my father pursed his lips.

"That's incredibly filthy, Rhonda."

I hung my head. "I know, Daddy."

My father placed a finger beneath my chin and lifted my head, and I trembled as he towered above me.

"I find it exciting," he whispered, staring into my soul.

And then, he cupped the back of my head, leaned forward, and kissed me gently on the lips. Warmth flooded my cheeks, and my heart hammered like a machine-gun.

Oh God help me! I thought deliriously, my legs threatening to give way.

My father pulled back and regarded me speculatively for a moment. I felt my mouth move without purpose as my senses whirled.

He smiled, this time not showing his teeth. He leaned forward and kissed me again, tenderly parting my lips with his tongue and searching for mine. His mouth now tasted fresh, as if he'd brushed before bed; with a desperate, brutish growl, I dropped the towel, threw my arms around his neck, and helplessly devoured him.

I savaged his tongue with mine, crushing my naked breasts against his hairy chest as I wildly ran my fingers through his hair. He matched my fumbling teenage ardor with a man's masculine maturity, wrapping me up in his arms so tightly I could scarcely draw breath.

"Rhonda," he choked, and we then moaned together.

He broke off the kiss, and I watched wide-eyed with wonder as he feasted his baby-blues upon my heaving boobs. He cupped them firmly, expertly thumbing my areolas and then pinching my nipples. White-hot urgency lanced through my body, slicing down through my tummy and settling deliciously into my loins.

"You have truly marvelous tits, Rhonda," my father said softly. "Just like your mother's. I can't wait to gobble them up."

Tits... I thought feverishly. *He called them tits...*

With my heart threatening to explode, I watched my father hungrily engulf one jiggling mammary with a satisfied groan. His tongue danced upon the areola and then the quivering nipple while I held his face against my chest and saw red dots mushroom behind my eyelids. He licked moisture from my cleavage before sucking on the other tit, lapping and slurping voraciously.

"That's right, Daddy," I whispered, experiencing an arousal so decadent it left me dizzy. "Suck your daughter's titties."

I cradled his head, heart pounding, listening to him grunt and smack, an incredible sense of intimacy flooding through me. I stroked his hair as he devoured my boobs, my flesh gleaming with his saliva. He took one enraged nipple between his teeth and firmly nipped, and pleasure so shocking nearly dropped me to the floor.

"Daddieeeeeee," I keened rapturously.

He reached between us, cupped my mound, and expertly flicked a finger on my clitty. Ecstasy rocked my loins, and I nearly wept with joy.

"Yessssss," I hissed, grunting, hips bucking.

But then, he stopped.

He stared at me for a long moment, and then sat me down on the bed. It was my turn to stare. The mammoth bulge had reawakened in his boxers, and I could see the outline of his knob pressed against the fabric. I hissed my impatience, undulating my greasy snatch on the mattress like a whore.

"Shhhhh," my father said softly, pressing a finger to my lips. "Hush, now."

His gleaming eyes seemed divorced from his face as he gently took my hand and pushed it through the opening in his shorts.

I inhaled sharply, awkwardly grasping a pulsating rail of muscle, marveling over the incredible hardness and heat that scorched my palm. I squeezed his shaft reflexively, and then stroked upward, feeling fat crinkly veins filled with pumping blood. My father bucked his hips and sucked in his breath.

"Rhondaaaaaaaaa," he groaned.

My fingers reached his tip, discovering a fat spongy helmet slicked with oily fluid. I squeezed it, and my father grunted his enjoyment. My degenerate coochie flexed with depraved excitement and I gasped for breath.

"Have you ever touched a hard cock before?" he demanded, staring down at me intently.

"No, Daddy," I whispered, my heart thundering.

"That's good," he said. "I had hoped to be your first." He

shifted, grunting again. "Pull down my shorts. I want you to see it."

I wanted to see it, oh yes I did. Moaning, I quickly peeled his boxers down his legs, and he kicked them aside.

I gazed up at him, unable to believe the natural beauty of his naked body -- his muscular hairy chest, his ridged belly, and his lean, firm legs. I'd just seen those things, of course, but this was different, as if he were now somehow unchained, and my senses spun madly.

And then, there was his *cock*, ominously jutting forth from his darkly stubbled groin, blunt and club-like, mere inches from my face. That part of him I'd never seen, and my lust increased to the point of madness.

Eagerly, I grasped his shaft again, stroking upward to its knob. The swollen bulb's skin was stretched shiny, taut like a glove, and I thought that it surely must hurt. I squeezed gently just below it; several clear gleaming beads abruptly dripped from his slit, and I could smell a primitive sexual fury that sinfully roiled my loins. When I imagined this thing inside of me, I nearly came unglued. I wondered briefly in my fervor if my father had a condom.

He purposefully stepped forward, and pressed his drooling glans against my cheek. Hot slimy juice smeared my flesh, and I gasped out loud. He rubbed his dribbling bulb against my lips, greasing them with milt.

"Open your mouth, Rhonda," he breathed.

For some reason, I hadn't expected this. When I hesitated, my father sucked in his breath.

"Right now, young lady," he hissed.

Once again, his stern tone demanded absolute compliance. Tentatively, I parted my lips upon his helmet. His effluence didn't taste as bad as I'd feared, and emboldened, I licked the slimy moisture like a kitten.

My father groaned, humping forward, and suddenly, my

warm piehole was filled with a succulent, jaw-popping mass. His fluid dribbled across my tongue, hot and slippery. I slurped him like a lollipop, slicking his knob with slobber.

"Cup my balls," my father croaked.

I fondled his scrotum -- the skin was wrinkled and downy-soft, and the balls were hot and firm in my palm.

"Squeeeeze them..." my father rasped.

I squeezed, and he gasped his approval.

"Put your other hand on my cock," he wheezed. "Stroke me and suck me at the same time..."

I did as I was told, my heart pounding. I wondered if he had been this aggressive with my mother, and so confident in what pleased him. He abruptly clasped the back of my head and pulled me forward, sinking his helmet into the back of my throat. I gagged, choking. He pulled back for a moment, gasping, and stared down at me.

"You'll get better with practice," he said softly. "Your mother did. Now, please continue."

I had a pretty good idea how to proceed -- I enjoyed watching computer porn and playing with myself.

I reapplied my lips and tongue, slurping and sucking, vigorously bobbing my head on his knob while I stroked his beefy bone, the nasty sounds I made with my drooling mouth both sloppy and wet. My father groaned blissfully, guiding my face with his hands, the visceral odor of his sweaty crotch igniting my rioting teenage hormones.

"Ohhhh baby baby baby..." he moaned.

My lusting heart surged with power. *I* now held dominion over *him* in this single heavenly moment, and he was enjoying every blessed second of it.

His hip thrusts quickened, growing stronger. When I looked up at him, I saw his head thrown back and his eyes closed, and I knew instinctively that he was about to climax.

Eagerly, I went down on him as best I could, relishing the

increased flow of lubrication on my tongue and the scorching heat of his helmet, awaiting something I could not yet fathom.

"Rhondaaa noooo..." he rasped, and pushed me back.

I stared at him silently, breathless with anticipation. He opened his eyes and gazed down at me unsteadily. His chest heaved and his throbbing cock glistened and dripped with my slobbers.

"I want you to see it..."

He spread his legs and took my hand, guiding my fingers to a moist secretive spot just behind his ballsack. He shivered urgently and firmly stroked his shaft.

"Press down hard," he hissed.

I pressed. My father inhaled sharply -- the flow of gleaming beads increased, his knobslit burbling like a stopped-up drain. Drizzling droplets spattered the tops of my tits, while he whined like an animal caught in a trap, and then stroked upward to his tip.

A thick pearly torrent abruptly cannonaded from his peehole, hurling end-over-end through the void between us. Another milky burst followed, more forcefully than the first; they lashed my lips and cheeks like warm pearly whips, salty and slimy and tasting strangely like fruit.

Grunting loudly, he put my hand on his shaft; *I* inhaled sharply, for the first time experiencing the muscular ferocity of a man's pulsating contractions. I gaped, awestruck, his gouting wads seemingly without end, leaving me dazed and dripping on the edge of the bed.

And then, he ceased, completely drained, panting hoarsely in the darkness and trembling. I felt his seed oozing down my face, and I moaned ecstatically, filled with joy that I had pleased him so totally.

He stared at me, and then chuckled exhaustedly.

"Wait here, baby girl."

I watched him disappear into the bathroom, heard water running in the sink a moment later. My head spun with what had just occurred. I envisioned his cock exploding like that inside me, and felt a thrill of excitement. Again I wondered if he had a condom somewhere, and shivered with anticipation. Soon, my father was going to make love to me and transform me into a woman.

When he returned, he was carrying a wet hotel hand towel. He knelt at the foot of the bed between my legs and gently wiped my face clean.

"Was it good for you, Daddy?" I whispered.

It was a silly question, but I had to ask. My father nodded.

"You're a natural, Rhonda."

My heart pounded. "As good as Mom?"

He frowned. "Don't compare yourself to her."

"Why not? That's all *you've* been doing."

He paused, as if realizing that fact for the first time. And then, he shook his head.

"You're better."

I knew he really meant it, and I thrilled to his praise. Finished, he pushed me down on the bed, spread my legs, and I felt my wrinkled slit gape wide with expectancy.

"Are we going to make love, Daddy?" I whispered hopefully.

"I'm going to get you ready first," my father replied.

I really had no idea what he meant, but it sounded delicious. When he pressed his stubbled cheek against the inside of my left knee and licked, I quivered, relishing the exquisite sensation.

"That's nice, Daddy."

"It gets better."

My father grasped my legs and spread them wide, and I purred my approval with uninhibited delight. He trailed his tongue up my inner left thigh, and I wriggled my rump, mewling with impatience. He reached my pussy and paused for a moment -- I watched him savor the sight of my mauve outer folds and the gleaming pink meat of my glistening center. He licked his lips and gazed up at me.

"Your pussy hair is so thick," he breathed. "So womanly..."

He rasped his fingers through my coarse dark ringlets, and then tugged gently. I squirmed, moaning. He spread my lips through my bush, exposing my erect, pulsing bud. I shuddered, writhing with expectation. My daddy was going to eat my virgin pussy, just like I'd seen in all those dirty movies. I felt my channel flex in response; a juicy stream gurgled forth from my seething pot and slicked my trembling inner thighs with honey.

"Daddieeee pleeeze..."

My father chuckled salaciously, and licked the sweetness from my flesh. I struggled, trying to hump my crotch against his face, but he held me at bay. Still chuckling, he gently probed my outraged clitty and fingered a small, delicate circle upon it. My heart trip-hammered painfully as an incredible white-hot spear impaled my agonized loins --

"Ahhhhieeeeeee!" I wailed deliriously, and exploded.

Hot juice geysered loudly upon my father's upturned face, and he slurped hungrily as he consumed it.

He clutched my bouncing bottom and squeezed my round moons, slowly drawing my humping loins to him, until I felt my dripping pubes brush his cheeks. I heard him inhale deeply the secretive odor of my cunt, while I twisted and moaned and grabbed up handfuls of sheets. And then, he tenderly, almost daintily, applied his tongue to my nubbin.

"Uhhhhhhhhfuuuck!" I grunted, and exploded again.

Gargling with approval, Daddy chewed my gristly morsel, feasting upon it while I rocked my hairy pelvis wantonly on his face. He licked my wrinkled labia and nosed-gouged my slit, tonguing my taint and breathing the sweaty stink of my bung. He pressed his face deep into my crack, relishing the odorous darkness between my cheeks. Unmindful of my cries, he pushed his nose into my rectum and simultaneously licked beneath it, and I wailed like a demon consumed in a blaze.

"Oh Daddieeeee!" I squealed crazily. *"Eat my dirty ass!"*

Suddenly overcome, my father fastened his mouth on my bunghole and sucked, delving deeply with his tongue. I capitulated to his plunderings with a violent wracking shudder, my tight slippery sphincter clamping down like a vise. When he slipped two fingers into my tortured pussy, I climaxed *again* with a shrill ecstatic cry, flooding his twisted features and nearly drowning him.

My father abruptly stood up at the end of the bed. His hair was drenched and his face glistened with my juices. He grabbed my ankles and jerked us close, rubbing his semi-erect dick against my wet puckered folds; I gasped, watching him harden fully.

He grasped his dripping meat, knob-popping my clitty with a moist lewd *splat!* Droplets flew upward, and I writhed helplessly. He did it again, and I mindlessly cried out. He ran his length up and down my puckered petals, the sensation so obscene I almost went insane.

"Get a condom, Daddy," I grunted roughly, shamelessly bucking my hips.

He stopped abruptly, staring at me with surprised realization.

"I don't have one, baby," he said softly.

I nearly screamed my frustration. I wanted my father's cock inside me -- I *needed* it inside me. But I didn't want to get pregnant when he ejaculated.

"It's a good thing you mentioned it," he murmured reflectively, still rubbing his knob in my folds.

"I guess you could always pull out," I whispered breathlessly. "I've heard of that."

He shook his head. "Sometimes there's sperm in a man's lubrication."

As if to prove his point, he squeezed behind his knob -- a long slippery string dangled from his peehole and pooled lubriciously in the matted ringlets blanketing my mound. The sight inflamed me further.

"Maybe you could *ask for one at the desk,*" I whined urgently, bucking my hips.

"That would be embarrassing, baby girl."

"Then a goddamn vending machine!"

"This isn't a truck stop."

I squirmed like a slut. *"I want you, Daddieee!"*

My father chuckled. "Control yourself, young lady."

He stretched out on top of me and pressed his face between my tits. He sucked on the side of one boob, and then the other, sending soft tingles through my chest and into my tummy. My nipples seemed as big as boulders as I rubbed them on his cheeks; he took one in his mouth and suckled tenderly. He tongued my areola and I inhaled sharply, shivering. And then he stared at me, smiling, and I felt something flutter in the pit of my tummy.

"I love you, Rhonda," he said softly.

"Oh, Daddy," I whispered, my heart beating hard. "I love you, too."

I pulled his face down to mine and slipped my tongue between his lips. We explored each other's mouths, moaning together. His lips became firm and demanding; my heart sped up and the quivering in my virgin pussy increased. I took his hand and guided it there, groaning as he caressed my folds. Daddy's dirty organ was a smoldering iron rail throbbing on my belly. I gazed between our bodies and watched knob juice seeping from the slit while he played with me.

"Daddy," I whispered, "Make sweet love to me."

"We can't," he said. "It's too dangerous without a condom."

"I don't care if I get pregnant," I whispered. "I don't care about anything anymore. I want you to be my first, and we may never get this chance again."

I watched his resolve crumble like old parchment. Tears filled his eyes, and my heart soared at the sight of them. He rolled aside, onto his back.

"I want you on top," he said. "That way, you can control things."

My love for him grew tenfold. He was thinking of my pleasure, not his own. He wanted this to be special -- for him and for me.

"All right, Daddy."

My father clutched his shaft and forced it up straight from his groin. I could see it pulsing, the knob glistening and oozing. I trembled with adrenaline, electrified by the forbidden, dangerous step I was about to take. My father grunted an acknowledgement; he sensed it, too. He squeezed his shaft, and droplets spurted from his slit, his palm sounding soft and squishy as he stroked. I stared, wide-eyed with fascination.

"I'm yours, Rhonda," my father breathed. "Fuck me like you own me."

Murmuring softly, I squatted above Daddy's cock and almost wept with joy. I felt my labia part and my slick portal widen, and I dripped my excitement onto his crotch. I positioned my puckered cunt upon his plump knob and rubbed tentatively, feeling my orifice widen further to accommodate his abundance. He didn't thrust; he allowed me to set the pace. My lips enfolded him in a warm, wet grapple; I gasped at the sensation and slid down a little more.

"Eeeeeeeee..." I keened gloriously. "It's soooo big, Daddieeee..."

I grunted, rapturously overwhelmed. My father's plentiful girth was exquisite, and my stretched walls surrounding it felt divine. He thrust gently, sinking additional inches into my willing young body.

"Ooooooooo yesssss..." I crooned.

"Am I hurting you?"

"Ooooo noooo..."

I was telling the truth. I had expected pain to accompany my loss of innocence, but there was none. Nor was there blood. I *did* experience a moment's resistance, but then it was done.

Encouraged, I wiggled my rump, sliding him deeper. My father offered me a satisfied grunt as he watched his shaft disappear into my channel. I moaned, my swollen pussy lips clutching and sucking moistly as they devoured the muscular rail.

Abruptly, I bottomed out with a bestial growl, my thighs gripping his waist, my cunt locked to his groin, and my knees sunk into the soaking-wet sheets.

"Jesus God, you're tight," my father hissed.

His voice seemed to come from another world. My head was thrown back and my eyes were closed, and sweat dripped off my chin into my cleavage. His meaty knob pushed insistently against the wall of my cervix as he grasped my thighs for leverage. I groaned mightily, and a sudden juicy gush squirted from my stretched pussy and drenched his crotch. His breathing, and mine, came in short ragged bursts.

"Are you all right?" my father croaked.

I nodded, unable to speak. Hesitantly, I lifted my rump all the way up to his tip, and then slowly slid back down. There were no words to describe how it felt.

"Ooooooooo," I crooned blissfully.

I did it again, and yet again, my senses spinning wondrously. I raised my hips a final time, and stared into his gleaming blue eyes.

"I think I'm ready, Daddy."

"Me, too," he said.

I dropped my yawning pussy down firmly on his molten pole -- with a wicked rump-smacking squelch that bounced our bodies on the mattress, my animalistic grunt echoing of the walls of the hotel bedroom.

"Do it!" my father exclaimed.

He grabbed my thighs and bucked, his heavy slick length violating my hot little hole. I dug my fingers into his shoulders and shrieked with an ardor unknown to me until that very moment, my ravishment complete.

I stared down at him -- his eyes were closed, but his mouth gaped wide as he gasped for breath. And then, he groaned in ecstasy, his fingers clenching my limbs so tightly that bruises darkened my flesh. I leveraged myself on his shoulders and powered down with my groin, until he was completely hilted once more and I was crucified on his cross.

"Oh God oh God oh God..." I mewled helplessly.

The bed rocked as I lewdly wriggled my loins, anointing his shaft like a priestess. When he opened his eyes and stared at me, I dropped my heavy tits across his face. He seized one swinging globe greedily and hungrily sucked the nipple. I delivered the other to his parted lips, his tongue a twisting serpent, while my hip thrusts quickened and the bedsprings squeaked. I sat up abruptly and began humping harder still, my ravaged cunt squishing moistly like cream in a French pastry.

"Fuck me, Daddieeee!" I hissed salaciously.

With a barbaric grunt, my father rammed his cock deep, and I inhaled sharply with pain and ecstasy. Together, we attained a rhythm, and our enraged thrusting became faster and stronger. My heavy tits flopped and my greasy hair flew. Our bodies ran with sweat as our groins slapped together, and our frenzied panting filled the room.

"Harder, Daddy! Fuck me harder!"

My father fucked me hard, grunting with the effort, his body sunk into the mattress, trapped beneath my weight. He reached up and clutched my bouncing tits, pinching my nipples and jerking a loud snort from my throat. I slid my hand down to where we were joined and rubbed my swollen bobbin with a lewd, lethal purpose.

"I'm cuuummminng Daddieee...!" I shrieked.

My cunt walls contracted furiously around his pounding manhood, my orgasm raging through me. My pussy exploded, showering him with juice. I leaned forward and braced myself as he continued to hammer his groin against mine, my prurient wails loud and continuous. I climaxed again, saturating his loins and the mattress beneath us --

My father flipped me onto my belly and unceremoniously hiked up my hips. I knew he intended to fuck me like a bitch in heat, and gloriously, I became just that. He rubbed his throbbing length back and forth in my crack, and I felt his flaming knob drooling lube on my bung. For one frightening second, he pushed firmly against my pooper --

"Nooo Daddieeee noooo!"

-- but then slid down to my portal and slipped just inside. Gratefully, I braced myself on my hands and knees, spread my legs wide, and he slammed his cock home with a single violent thrust, driving the solid pole deep and smashing my cervix like a battering ram.

I shrieked.

My father clutched my buttcheeks and squeezed them firmly.

"Your momma liked this, too," he rasped.

He gave a brutal thrust that rocked my body and slammed the headboard into the wall. He pulled out and sank back in, and then increased his tempo. He slapped my bouncing bottom as our bodies pounded together, the power and timing of his thrusts insanely overwhelming. My pussy squelched like a sodden sponge and my titties flopped heavily as he ravaged my inferno with a purpose not of this world.

"Oh God Daddy fuck me fuck me!"

My father grabbed my hips and split me in half. Another orgasm loomed ominously -- I wasn't sure I could take it, but I wanted it just the same.

"Finger me, Daddy..." I huffed, nearly spent. *"I'm almost there..."*

My father reached around, searching roughly between my legs. He found my clitty and probed, and a bolt of blue lightening crackled through my crotch and down my shuddering legs. I gasped for breath, the raw reality of our coupling slippery and rank. He probed me again, and I finally exploded with a scorching wail of release, my mind and muscles twitching and squirming like a basketful of snakes.

"I'm cuummming!" Daddy howled, like the beast that he was.

His erection swelled hugely inside me, and I cried out as his first manly jet blasted deep into my channel. He grabbed my buttcheeks and pulled me fast against his groin, holding me in place as he grunted and strained. He delivered wad after wad into my churning cauldron, his scalding issuance combining with mine and running down the backs of my thighs and puddling on the mattress. And then, we collapsed together, my face buried into a pillow, the sound of our exhausted breathing filling my ears.

"God help me, Rhonda," he gasped.

His lean hard body pressed me flat on the bed, imprisoning me with warmth, and I felt his amazing manhood slowly deflating inside me. He kissed the side of my neck, and I crooned with contentment.

And then, he rolled aside. We both heard my pussy fart loudly and wetly, and we chuckled together in the silence. I snuggled up close and lay my head on his chest, my fingers idly curling the hair around his nipples.

"Do you think we made a baby?" I murmured.

He sighed.

"I don't know. Maybe." He paused. "Are you worried?"

"No."

I knew I had a choice if that situation arose.

"What's going to happen now?" I whispered. "Between us?"

"Whatever you decide, baby girl."

"You've spoiled me, Daddy," I breathed, "for any other man."

"You've spoiled me, too."

I hugged him, and then kissed his lips. He ran his hands down my spine and cupped my tacky bottom. I wrinkled my nose, the rancid stink of our sex overpowering. He chuckled when he saw me wince.

"It's not funny, Dad. We smell gross. Can we take a shower?"

"Sure."

I ran my hand down his chest and flopped his limp, sticky organ.

"I want us all cleaned up so we can get dirty again."

He groaned softly. "Don't expect too much. I'm pretty worn out."

I grinned wickedly. "I know a way to get you going again." I pecked him on the mouth. "You said it yourself -- I'll get better with practice."

THE END
Get Access to over 20 more FREE Erotica Downloads at Shameless Book Deals

SHAMELESS BOOK DEALS is a website that shamelessly brings you the very best erotica at the best prices from the best authors to your inbox every day. Sign up to our newsletter to get access to the daily deals and the Shameless Free Story Archive!

STEP INSIDE MY HEART - KARLY DALTON

Zoey had just turned eighteen. Now a beautiful woman she knew what she truly wanted. What she needed.

Jake was a force to be reckoned with. A man's man that few women could resist. Zoey was desperate for him. Her fertile body desperately ached for an unprotected encounter. He filled her thoughts and dreams. The only problem, Jake was her Step. Was it wrong to feel so right? Could she do anything to make her fantasies a reality?

~

I used to think I was pretty normal. I mean, I think I'm pretty normal. Most of the time. In most ways, I'm just like any other girl. I like girl stuff. I like makeup. I like shopping. I like hanging out with my friends. I like bad TV shows about stupid stuff. And I cry when I watch puppies and kittens because they're so freaking cute I can't take it! *OMG! How could you not cry? Are you a monster?!*

But I guess I'm not normal in *every* way. I don't really

know how to say this. I don't even really like admitting it to myself. I don't think I can tell anybody, not even my best friend. I don't even like thinking about it. I don't want to say it out loud. I'm afraid that once I say it, it becomes real.

But it's like most things, if you don't like something about yourself, or you think you're weird, you can't help but think about it all the time. *Don't think about a pink elephant!* It's impossible not to.

It becomes like an obsession. You want it to stop but it just won't. And the more you try to make it go away, the more it forces itself up into the front of your mind.

I try not to think about it, but I can't help myself. It's supposed to be wrong, or is it wrong? I don't know. *Why is it wrong anyway?* I'm only eighteen. How am I supposed to know what's wrong and what's right? It's not like I want to rob a bank or murder somebody! I'm not a bad person. At least I don't think I am.

What's a girl supposed to do? I'm only human after all.

Not to be cliché, but Jake's the definition of tall, dark and handsome. He has the body of an athlete from years of college sports. But he's no dumb jock. He's got a high-paying job at a tech firm, and is one of those people who is comfortable in his own skin. He's easy to talk to, makes you laugh, and is easy to like. Oh, and I *love* the scruff on his beautiful face.

I'm watching him do his morning exercise routine. Pushups, pull ups, sprints. He does it every morning, and every morning I can't help but watch. I try not to drool. His abs are chiseled from granite and I stare hypnotized as beads of sweat glisten and flow over the muscles of his perfect body.

When he's finished, he showers, and if I'm being honest, I have to admit that I sneak peeks when I can get up the courage. Glistening beads of water washing over every muscle, every inch of his rock-hard body. It's almost too much to take. The one time I saw his manhood it made me so wet I couldn't stop myself from masturbating. I think of it all the time now.

Once, I think he saw me creeping on him, but he never mentioned it. He'd never embarrass me like that. He's my step-dad after all.

~

OKAY, I'll just say it because I'm sure you already figured it out and I'm sick of denying it. *I want my step-daddy.* I want him so badly it's driving me crazy. I don't know why.

I know it's unusual, which also makes it a turn-on because it's taboo. Why do people get so damned turned on by things they're not supposed to? There must be something in our DNA. We're programmed to get excited and, in my case, wet when something is forbidden.

I have mixed feelings about it. Part of me knows it's wrong, or at least weird. Part of me is excited that it's wrong. Part of me thinks it makes total sense.

Who wouldn't want to sleep with a gorgeous older man who makes you feel safe and buys you stuff? And has the body of a Greek god!? I'd be crazy *not* to have feelings for my step-daddy.

I'd dated a few guys in high school, but there wasn't much to it. I just wasn't feeling them. They were fine just kind of silly. They felt like friends not lovers. I wanted to be "normal" and have feelings for them, I just didn't have them. I tried but I needed more. I needed Daddy.

Ugh. It's so frustrating to want something so badly that you're not supposed to want. Or shouldn't have? Or could I? I don't even know. It's all too confusing. To be cliché again, how could something that feels so right be wrong?

I don't have any idea why Mom ever left him. I think she cared more about her career than anything else. I barely see her anymore now that I've turned eighteen. It was like, "Happy birthday. You're an adult now. Here's a cupcake and a hundred bucks. I have to go close a business deal in Sweden."

The funny thing is I didn't mind. I respected her work ethic, and she wasn't a bad mom. She was just kind of obsessed with working. Not to mention her frequent trips over the years had given Jake and I plenty of alone time together. We'd never done anything, but I'd developed more than a crush over the years. He was always fun to hang out with. Always made awesome dinners. A man's man who cooks! That rare creature still exists! And he's in the house!

One time he made this elaborate fish paella because he knew how much I loved it. I'd had it for the first time at a friend's birthday dinner and had come home raving about this magical new food. So what did Step-Daddy do? A few weeks later he made me the best freaking paella I've ever had! He could open his own restaurant!

Mom was away on another business trip and I hated to admit it but was kind of glad. I had Jake to myself again. Dinner was amazing. It felt like we were a married couple. I fantasized about our life together. All the things we'd do, the places we'd go. How did Mom ever leave? I just didn't get it.

When he ended the meal with homemade apple crumble for dessert, I almost had an orgasm! OMG it was so good. And the sparkle in his eye when he saw how much I liked it drove me crazy. He wanted to make me happy.

Suddenly, I was struck with an overwhelming desire I'd never had before. It hit me like a ton of bricks. My whole being ached, from my toes to me core.

I wanted a baby. *His baby.* I wanted to get pregnant and have a baby with this man. *Stupid teenager!* I forced myself to stop thinking of such things. I was only eighteen. I had stuff to do. College. Car loans. The usual. This was no time to be getting pregnant. Especially not by my step-daddy! Still, if I'm being totally honest, part of me enjoyed the fantasy.

Jake even taught me basic life stuff like changing my oil. Every time I save fifty bucks on an oil change I smile. Not only was he my protector but he taught me some self-defense.

"You need to be able to protect yourself out there. Just in case," he said when he showed me some basic martial arts. And when he taught me how to flip him to the ground, and I landed on top of him, straddling him, my thighs got all wet and warm.

I always wondered if he felt the heat on his stomach as I struggled not to push myself down to his groin and start rubbing my mound on him.

This man was invading my mind. It was hard to stop fantasizing about him. The more I tried to be "normal" and date regular guys my age, the more it made me want Jake. They just could never measure up. They never made me feel so safe and secure. They never seemed like *men*. They were mostly oversexed dorks who seemed to care more about getting in my pants than taking care of me or sharing a life together.

Part of it might be my own fault. I mean, not my fault but nature's fault. I couldn't help that I was given large, perky breasts and long, lean legs. Evidently, I was also too cute. I have huge, wide blue eyes that everyone says makes me look like an anime kitten. I'm not complaining at all, but it was hard sometimes at school because most guys stared at my tits all day long. Even some odd teacher. Though they at least hid it better. Sometimes my classmates even said some pretty gross things about what they wanted to do on my innocent face. Ugh. Gross. I'm not some sex freak looking to get jizzed on by horny guys. I want a connection.

Don't most women? Isn't that normal? Jeez, I think there's just too much porn in the world. How about some intimacy?

I'm not cold-hearted. I can see how tough it must be to be a teenage guy with raging hormones, and all you have to do is click once, and suddenly there's a billion sexy women doing things you can't even imagine! It would be like if I walked into a shoe store and everything was free! I'd lose it for sure. Still, that wasn't the kind of relationship I was looking for. Especially since I'd been treated so well for so long by Jake. I knew what a relationship should be like. The problem was he happened to be my step-dad. Why does life do that crap? It's too much!

I knew I had it bad when one night I was really trying to masturbate to this fantasy about Bryan, a cute guy from school. I mean I was really trying. He was really cute and had a great body. He was on the swim team and I remember the image of his long muscular body gliding through the cool pool waters. It made me feel a small tingle, so when the time came I tried to use the moment. Only of course it didn't work. I just couldn't really get aroused. I wanted to, but there wasn't much going on inside. After a while I decided to just give up and try again another time, frustrated I couldn't even figure out how to masturbate right. Maybe I did need to watch some porn after all.

So I was just about to call it a night and go to sleep, but just before I got to my room, I heard Jake on the phone in the other room. I don't remember what he was talking about. It was something boring and meaningless like bills or renewing our cable, but suddenly I was wet. Really wet. His deep soft voice sent tingles through my body and I couldn't stop my fingers from doing what they wanted. It wasn't long before I was trying to keep myself from moaning too loudly. Step-Daddy's voice was driving me crazy. I played with myself as I listened to him, and the next thing I knew I was having one of the most intense orgasms of my life.

Afterwards I felt a little guilty about it, but it didn't stop me from doing it again. And again.

~

MOM HAD BASICALLY LEFT me the house. She owned it of course but was never there. She'd gotten a promotion (and I was proud if her) but it meant she was around even less than usual. I'm sure it had a lot to do with why she and Jake eventually split. He needed more attention. A relationship can't work when people are so far away for so long. Maybe it works sometimes like with military people who go away then come back, but they come back for long periods of time. Mom was never home for more than a couple of days before she jetted off for weeks at a time. I doubted she cheated, she didn't seem the type, but it was hard to imagine she didn't. I couldn't believe Jake didn't. By the time they split it was like they were buddies who saw one another once every few months. How could they not cheat on each other?

Jake had moved out months ago but luckily had remained in town. When I first heard he was leaving it was like someone had kicked me in the stomach. I had so many mixed feelings. Sadness, anger at Mom, and desire to be with him. I wanted to go live with him but that's not what people do. Kids don't live with their step-parents when they get divorced or whatever. That would be weird. Especially since I had such an intense crush on my step-daddy. That definitely wouldn't go over well.

Jake and I still spent time together but I missed him. I missed his dinners and lessons and our talks. My raging teen hormones really missed drooling over his morning workouts.

Finally, I couldn't take it anymore. The buildup was too much. I was going crazy. I had to get my feelings off my chest. I might run away crying after I did it, but I just had to tell Jake how I felt. I had to know if maybe—just *maybe*—he felt the same way.

I invited him over to dinner and tried to cook the paella. I was hoping it would remind him of that great night we had. Maybe he'd get the idea. Maybe he'd just think I was a stupid girl with a crush.

I was so nervous I burned pretty much everything, and when he got there was no food, just the smell of burnt rice in the air. He smiled like he appreciated the attempt I made and ordered us some pizza. *There you go again taking care of me.*

We caught up on the small talk, which I could barely concentrate on because my heart felt like it was going to jump out of my throat the entire time. I kept thinking, *Tell him how you feel. Tell him. He'll understand. Maybe he feels the same way.*

No, don't tell him you dope! He's a grown man, you're a teenage girl. He's your step-daddy!

Tell him. Don't tell him! I thought my head was going to explode by the second slice of pizza.

"There's something I've been wanting to tell you for a long time," I blurted out of nowhere.

"What is it?" he asked.

"It's sort of embarrassing," I said. Just putting the idea out there made my heart thump like a hammer. I hoped he didn't notice the ruby-red flush in my face.

"I thought we could talk about anything," he replied.

Did he have any clue what I was really trying to say? Or did he think I was going to tell him about being dumped or fired or something "normal." Part of me hoped he knew. I hoped he noticed me blossoming over the years, but I couldn't be sure.

I wanted to just say it, but you know how it is when people are too scared to say what they really mean? So they try to give clues without actually saying "it." That way they can always pretend they had no idea, if it turns out they were wrong.

Daddy wasn't about to come right out and admit he might have feelings for me. I knew he was too conservative to put that out there. I was scared. I didn't want to ruin our relationship. But I wanted more. I wanted it so badly I just had to take the risk. So I guess if anyone was going to put it out there it had to be me. I gulped, took a big breath and just laid it out there naked for everyone to see. *Please don't blow up in my face or I'll go running out of the room crying*, I thought.

"Okay, here it is…I've been fantasizing about you forever," I finally said after some hemming and hawing.

There, I said it. It's out in there in the universe.

Now it was Daddy's turn to be uncomfortable. His face went red, and I could tell what I said had affected him.

"I don't think we should talk about that kind of stuff," he replied.

"But you always said I could talk to you about anything."

"But this isn't right."

"Doesn't that sort of make it more exciting?" I asked.

His eyes widened at my comment and I could tell by the sparkle in his eyes that at least part of him agreed, even if he didn't want to admit it.

"You're right," I said, "It's not about talking." And then I just held my breath and kissed him.

His soft warm lips sent waves of electricity through my body. It was better than I had even imagined. Our tongues touched, I felt Jake's passion, and then he pulled back.

"Zoey, what are you doing?"

I smiled half embarrassed, half aroused. "Like they say. Actions speak louder than words. I've been wanting to do that since...well since forever!"

"Okay, well, I don't think we should...."

But I'd already gone this far, there was no turning back now. I'd rather be an embarrassed fool than not try to get what I truly wanted. And now that we had kissed, every iota of my being wanted Daddy more than it ever had. Reality was even better than the fantasy. I *had* to have Daddy. At least, I had to give it my best try, or I'd never forgive myself. My teen body was on overload. My hormones and heart were exploding, taking control of everything.

I kissed him again. This time my tongue sliding deep into his mouth, pressing my large breasts against his muscular chest. My nipples erect and rubbing on Daddy's strong body. My hand instinctively went to his groin. My young brain might not know what to do to get Daddy to want me but my body did.

"Zoey," he muttered as he tried to push me back, but I could feel that his heart wasn't in it. I stroked the outside of his pants. Daddy moaned, then went rock hard in my hands. I smiled big because I knew Daddy wanted me too.

"Please, Daddy," I whimpered, and the yearning in my voice must have done something to Jake. Suddenly all of his protests were gone and he was transformed into a creature of passion. He pressed his lips hard against mine. His tongue passionately darted into my mouth. We wrapped our arms around one another and embraced in a passionate kiss.

His hands went to my thighs and it set my body aflame with desire.

I moaned as the warm wetness engulfed my core. I was preparing for Daddy. My body was readying itself. I needed him now.

My legs parted without my brain telling them to and his

hand slipped between my thighs. I knew he could feel my heat and it made me even wetter.

When his hand gently touched my groin I almost exploded. His fingers gently stroked my mound and I practically came right then and there. His fingers explored my center, tracing the outline of my folds and then making their way beneath the fabric of my shorts. My heart quickened. He was getting so close to my being!

Please, Daddy, please touch my flesh. I'm so hot and wet for you. I've never been so hot and wet. Please, Daddy, touch me!

It was like he read my mind, because at that moment his fingers pulled back the fabric of my panties and touched my flesh. He slid into the wetness of my folds, touching the entrance to my core. I tried to control myself but my body was in a frenzy. My thighs opened for him and my hips moved forward aching for his finger to enter me. *Oh, Daddy, I want you inside me so badly!*

I moaned and wiggled as he caressed me. He touched my clit and I shot into the heavens! I needed him now. My hand urgently opened his pants, searching for his warm flesh. When I felt him my eyes went wide. He was so thick and hard. And it was all for me. He wanted me. Daddy's thick cock wanted me badly. I felt it throbbing as I wrapped my hand around it. It barely fit! I'd never felt a cock so thick and hard before. I stroked it slowly and Daddy moaned for me. It made me so wet that his finger slipped inside me and I moaned with him. Together we explored each other's bodies with our hands, me stroking Daddy's big thick cock, while his finger slid deep inside my soaking wet core.

It felt like forever but was only a few moments before I couldn't take it any longer. I didn't know what the hell I was doing but my body knew it needed Daddy's cock inside me. My soaking wet pussy was screaming for Daddy's cock.

I pulled his pants down and the giant shaft popped out, stiff and ready.

He tore my wet panties and, before they were even off, my legs were spread wide, waiting, aching, for him to enter me.

He paused for a moment. "I need a condom," he said leaning over towards a drawer where he must have kept them. A sense a panic engulfed me. I didn't want anything between us. I needed his pure flesh against mine. I needed us to be one!

He opened the drawer and began searching.

I had to do something fast. Luckily, my body knew what to do. Even at my young age my body knew. I just needed to listen to my body not my brain. I knew he should wear a condom. I knew I could get pregnant. I knew I should be careful. But I didn't care. Not only didn't I care, I also wanted him naked inside me. I wanted to feel his hot seed pulse in my fertile body. I wanted his baby. *Get me pregnant daddy*, I thought. *Give me your baby!*

He grabbed a condom and began opening the package.

That's when both of my hands wrapped around his massive cock and pulled it to the opening of my being. I rubbed his hard head against my wet folds and he got even harder! How was that even possible? His head throbbed against my clit then slid to my opening and pulsed like a desperate beast.

He tried to control himself. "Baby, let me put on a…"

I arched back and opened myself completely. The tip of his manhood slid inside just a little.

"Oh, baby," he moaned.

"Oh, Daddy," I cooed, my hips slowly working his head deeper into me.

His huge cock spread my tight young pussy wider. I

ached so badly for it to be deeper I thought I was going to explode.

"Deeper, Daddy, deeper!" I begged.

I looked into his eyes with a yearning I'd never felt before. "Please, Daddy," I begged again.

And then it happened.

Something changed in his expression. He suddenly looked so intense, so filled with lust. I instantly got so wet I felt myself soaking his cock. My pleading and aching and writhing had made something click inside him. It made him want to fuck his little girl.

"Fuck me, Daddy," I pleaded.

And then, suddenly, he grabbed my ass and plunged his thickness to my core.

Shock waves shot through every fiber of my being as his hard cock spread me open. He drove deep into my very core and I gave in. My body and mind were all his. I was Daddy's girl and he could do whatever he wanted to me.

His thickness stretched me, but I pulled him even deeper. I wanted him in me as far as he could go. I wanted every inch of his throbbing cock.

His balls slapped against my ass as he fully entered me and we became one. He bucked and writhed inside my wetness, grabbing my tight ass and thrusting deeper than I thought possible.

"Oh yes, fuck me, Daddy!"

And he did. He fucked me hard. Pumping his shaft in and out like a jack hammer.

In and out.

In and out.

Thick and hard.

He pumped faster and faster.

He fucked me until I climaxed all over his rock-hard shaft. I'd never done that with a man before, and I didn't think anyone could ever make me cum that hard again. Except he did.

Before I could ever recover he was deep inside me again. Filling me with his massive cock. I felt his balls go hard when they touched me, and I knew daddy was going to cum.

"Cum in me, Daddy," I pleaded, grabbing his hard ass and pulling him into me. I wanted to feel his heavy balls unload their seed into my being.

"Cum, Daddy, cum in me!" I pleaded, aching to feel his hot seed.

He moaned loudly then arched his back and started fucking me so hard I lost all sense of the world. I was engulfed in ecstasy. His cock pounded me. Every thrust sending waves of pleasure from my toes to my head. I couldn't take much more of it. It was too much pleasure! But I needed more. I needed Daddy's seed.

I stroked his cum-filled balls and begged him again.

"Cum, Daddy. Cum in your good little girl."

His cock plunged all the way in and went rock hard. Then it started to spasm and I knew it was happening. I wanted his seed so badly I started to have another orgasm. My hips bucking and writhing wildly on his shaft as he shot every drop of warm seed into me. *"Yes, Daddy! Yes! Give me all your cum!*

I milked his balls with my tight pussy until he emptied himself and I had every drop inside me.

When it was over we laid in each other's arms. Sweaty and exhausted, I was content. I couldn't stop myself from smiling. I'd finally gotten what I'd wanted for as long as I could remember. And it was better than I had ever imagined. Sometimes the reality is even better than the fantasy. And I was grateful. And maybe pregnant with Daddy's baby.

THE END

Get Access to over 20 more FREE Erotica Downloads at Shameless Book Deals

SHAMELESS BOOK DEALS is a website that shamelessly brings you the very best erotica at the best prices from the best authors to your inbox every day. Sign up to our newsletter to get access to the daily deals and the Shameless Free Story Archive!

THE TEACHER'S NEW BRAT - ELIZA DEGAULLE

Alyssa's world was about to be turned upside down when she learns who the man of the house is...

Alyssa's Calculus teacher, Mr. Ford is a tough nut to crack. He seems relentless, and none of her charms seem to work on him. That is until she suddenly learns that Mr. Ford is destined to become the new man of her house. Thinking she can use the new sudden relation they share to her advantage, she quickly finds out Mr. Ford isn't going to be swayed so easily. If he's going to break the rules for Alyssa, he wants something in return - and that's everything Alyssa's purity and fertility can give him.

My brain hurt.
Like, it wasn't a headache.
My brain legitimately hurt.
I'd spent the last two hours trying to get a hold of all this calculus stuff. I thought I was good enough at math, but

apparently I had run into the limits of what I could comprehend.

I had lingered longer than most on Mr. Ford's lessons.

Maybe it was because none of it stuck. Maybe it was just because for a math teacher who was twenty years older than me, Mr. Ford was pretty damned hot.

Walking home through the night, I wondered why my mind slipped back to such a thought so easily. Perhaps it was just thinking of dirty fantasies with my teacher was far more preferable than trying to solve anything using trigonometric substitution.

That dark hair of his, those thick arms that told you he was far from the pencil-neck geek-type associated with his profession. That square jaw. Damn, I didn't usually have crazy older man fantasies, but if I ever wanted to seduce one of my teachers, he would definitely be at the top of the list.

He was a bit of a stick in the mud though. I doubted he even entertained dirty thoughts of doing things with his students.

Despite all that, I was looking forward to getting home. Getting some dinner. Maybe eating some ice cream fast because brain freeze was preferable to the pain school was putting me through.

I read something somewhere that said being relaxed is vital to succeeding on exams, and given I had Mr. Ford's final tomorrow, well, I guess I had better try to be relaxed.

Even if I felt absolutely hopeless that I could succeed at the test anyway.

Stopping outside my mother's house, I spotted something quite unusual.

Two cars. My mom had been my single parent ever since the man who was supposed to be responsible for my existence took off with another woman. She'd been most solitary since.

The other car wasn't mine, unfortunately.

God, why did Mom tell me I needed to get a B on all my finals for her to get me a car of my own?

I was eighteen years old. I was supposed to be an adult, for crying out loud. I couldn't be hitching rides from her forever. And with how little I was grasping calculus, I wasn't going to be able to meet her ultimatum.

Really, I was curious just who our visitor was.

The door was unlocked, and I walked right into the living room, and I almost crapped my pants at what I saw.

My mother was sitting there, smiling, and with a man's arm over her shoulder.

That man?

My calculus teacher, Mr. Ford.

"Um.... uh... did I come home too early?" I murmured, not even knowing what I was possibly suggesting.

"Alyssa, dear," my mom said, softly smiling in her undeniable Mom-ishness. "We have a lot to discuss, dear. You should sit down."

I did just that, hitting our armchair like I was a sack of bricks and putting my backpack down beside me. "I guess you want to explain why my calculus teacher is here?"

"I knew she would react like this," my teacher said, shaking his head.

"Well, this is why we wanted to be sure before telling her, didn't we?" my mom replied.

"Yes."

"Be sure of what?"

"Um, Alyssa, honey," my mom kept her smile up, clearly afraid of her words upsetting me. "Ian and I, uh.... um... we're getting married."

I did the natural response to such a thing.

I glared at her. I glared at Mr. Ford.

"Married? As in, a wedding? As in, Mr. Ford is going to be my dad?" I blinked. "Step-dad?"

"Alyssa, I'm not seeing where you could interpret this another way," Mr. Ford said. Or *Dad* said. I didn't even know what I should have labeled him mentally anymore. "I've been seeing your mother covertly for the past year. Lisa has brought joy to me I never thought possible, yet I knew that as your teacher it could prove difficult, so we kept it all a secret."

I glared at my mother. "You're marrying my teacher. Seriously?"

My mother just nodded. "I know it's sudden. We had a lot to discuss before we agreed to it. It's not something we take lightly dear. I just hope that you can learn to understand and accept our relationship."

Looking back and forth between them, the shock was slowly fading. I shouldn't have been so surprised. It wasn't like my mother wasn't a woman with desires of her own, and Mr. Ford didn't stop existing just because I wasn't in his classroom. He was a handsome man, right around my mother's age. He was absolutely perfect, especially given that charm and intellect he had.

Still, though, the fact that Mr. Ford was soon going to be my step-dad. It was really nuts.

Especially with how poorly I was doing in his class.

My mom reached out to me, taking my hand into hers, and her others on Mr. Ford's. "I want nothing more than for you to get along. I know I can't expect you to fully accept Ian as your stepfather, but it would mean the world to me if things weren't sour between you two."

"Why would it be? You think I can't be an adult, Mom?"

"Alyssa," Mr. Ford cut in. "Don't play oblivious. I know how poorly you've been doing in class recently. Your mother feels you're going to take your potential failure as a reason to resent me."

"Um, uh," I shook my head. "No, no, if I fail, it's my fault, it's nothing to do with you, Mr. Ford...err... Ian...err... Daddy?" I raised an eyebrow, completely unable to parse what I was supposed to call him now.

He laughed. "You can call me Ian outside the classroom. Just act as you normally would in class, Alyssa. My shifting marital status shouldn't interfere with our pupil and teacher relationship."

"Uh huh."

He took his time composing himself. "I know it's weird. I'll order us all some pizza tonight on me. You're my family now, and I'm going to do my damnedest to treat both of you right."

My mother smiled and leaned onto his shoulder. Ever so subtly, I could detect an uncertainty about her.

Why was she so worried? Yeah, it was a bit of a shock, mainly because it came out of nowhere. Did she think so lowly of her own daughter that she thought I'd flip out over her marrying one of my teachers?

There couldn't have been more to all of this, could there?

∽

"No way. No flipping way. Your new step-dad is Mr. Ford?"

"Why would I lie about something like this, Nikki?"

"I don't know, it's just so.... random."

Sighing, I stretched out onto the bed. Nicole was my long-time best friend, and the first person I went to to talk things through. The advice that she gave was never the best, but it was another mind to put on it all.

"So, them not telling you. How you taking it?" she asked.

"I can see why they waited. Wish they waited until I had already taken the final, though."

"Why?"

"Well, however long this marriage lasts, be it months or decades, it's going to be terribly awkward if my new step-dad is the reason I didn't get into the colleges I wanted because he failed me on an exam I'm probably going to legitimately fail anyway."

"He's just doing his job, you know?"

"Yeah, yeah, I tell myself that, but it puts pressure on me. I don't want to seem like I'm getting favoritism if someone finds out our sudden relation."

She paused a moment. "Why?" she echoed herself.

"Isn't it obvious? Oh, Alyssa only passed because her stepfather made her pass. What a terrible rumor to spread around."

"That's not the case though, right?"

"That's what I mean."

"Then you have nothing to worry about. Let stupid people think stupid things, Alyssa. That's why they're stupid to begin with." I shook my head smirking as she did something on her end, sipping some beverage. "Although I don't think you should give a shit even if he helps you."

"Hmm?"

"Nepotism is rampant all over society, Alyssa." Oh boy, here she goes again. She was hoping to be some sort of social sciences person, so she read a lot and had opinions. Lots of opinions. "It's just part of being human. This is your networking opportunity."

"What, you think I should just ask him to give me a good grade without me even trying?"

"Why not? Everyone you're competing against for a degree I bet is absolutely using everything they have to get the scholarship. This isn't the hill to die on, Alyssa. If you want to say you don't want to take advantage of your status, please, don't let me start."

"Alright, alright, just don't start going on about privilege and all that." I didn't dispute her words. "It's kinda moot. Mr. Ford isn't exactly the sort to go that hard against the rules. We joked that he has a stick up his ass, remember?"

"Yeah, we called him the sexiest asshole hard-ass teacher in the school. He could have been a model or a math teacher, and he's the kind of jerk who preferred the latter."

I didn't need to think of him like that right now. "He's going to be my step-dad, Nikki. Chill."

"Hot step-dad, huh? That doesn't push it off the table."

My eyes were wide at her words. "You're insane and are reading too many books that have absolutely nothing to do with your education."

"What I do underneath my covers with my phone in one hand is completely up to me, I'll have you know."

"You don't have to tell me about it, though."

"Don't act like you weren't giggling like a school girl talking about that stuff with me, Alyssa."

"That was before I knew he was going to be my step-dad!"

"Look, I get it. Just... roll with what life gives you, Alyssa. If he's going to fudge a grade for you, let him. He doesn't want to fail his new stepdaughter any more than you want to fail. I highly doubt he wants to enter this new relationship with you on a sour note. He wants everything to go swimmingly and wonderful. Nothing is in a vacuum, just remember that. Mr. Ford is a man with his own thoughts, wishes, and desires, no matter how much I... and you, for that matter, objectify him."

"It's just..." I was struggling to come up with a good counter.

"What? Roll with it. You got a sexy step-dad who can fix your whole suck at calculus problem. Embrace it, girl."

My mind immediately flashed back to that conversation on the sofa with him. How Mom wanted nothing more than for us to get along. How she wanted us to love one another, and be family.

A smile curled onto my lips. She was totally right. Mr. Ford, Ian, Daddy, whatever, he wanted to make sure I approved of him marrying my mother. There was nothing he wanted more.

Suddenly I felt a whole lot more powerful. "You're really good at opening my eyes sometimes, Nikki."

"Damn right I am." She laughed. "I hate to cut this short, but I really should be getting to sleep. Some of us can't guilt trip Step-Daddy into passing us in our classes. You should get some sleep too. Just in case he decides to go hard-ass on you, you know."

"Alright, alright. I'll see you tomorrow then."

"Right." The phone call ended.

I put the thing to the side, and stretched out once more. I was feeling a whole lot less stressed. She was right. I had networking to succeed with. I didn't have the money that Monty Megabucks would have, and their parents would buy a library for the school to make sure their kid got into Harvard. I was just playing with the hand I was dealt.

There was definitely something sexy though about having an older hunk like Mr. Ford under my finger though.

If only I had any clue who was really in control.

∽

THE CLOCK WAS TICKING BY. I was going through the exam, doing my work, putting in my best effort at answering it. Showing a little pride. Even if I knew I could badger "Daddy" into a good grade, maybe I'd pass anyway and could save the puppy dog eyes for something else.

Like a nicer car.

Still, I can't say I didn't waste a lot of time leaning forward, my chin resting on my hand and looking toward him. There was definitely something about him. Had he been working out more? I hated that I was suddenly jealous of my mother. The guys she had dated didn't hold a candle to Mr. Ford. It was really no wonder why he was the one she wanted to tie the knot with. He was definitely a guy you got in your grasp and never let go.

I imagined him running his hand through my hair, touching me so sensually. I shuddered a bit.

It was completely stupid of me, but I guess I was just a stupid overly romantic virgin.

Getting myself flustered, I tried to restore my focus.

It wasn't terribly effective.

Powering through, the time drew to a close and I had to just be happy with what I had right there.

Everyone was handing in their exams, and I was no different. I may have lingered behind everyone else, wanting to maybe say something charming or sexy, something that would say I would appreciate if he were really, really lenient with my grade. Something that would be private from the rest of the class at least.

The population of the class soon thinned out, and I started to make my journey to the front of the room.

He was looking my way as I approached. The last student besides me filed out as I reached him and handed him my exam. "Here it is," I said, trying to sound cute. "Go easy on me, wouldn't you?"

Mr. Ford took my test from me.

To my surprise, he opened it and immediately started going over it.

"I figure I'll just review yours and get you your grade as soon as possible, Alyssa."

"Oh?" I raised an eyebrow. I wasn't expecting this. "I wasn't expecting special treatment."

"It can't be avoided, can it? I'm marrying your mother. I can try to be professional, but I want to make sure you succeed all the same."

He went down the list. He was shaking his head, something that wasn't a good sign for me.

"I'm going to be honest here Alyssa. Your work leading up to here wasn't inspiring a whole lot of hope in me. The work here isn't doing much to prove me wrong."

Damn, so I really did bomb as horribly as I thought I was going to. I really was hoping I was just a bundle of nerves for no good reason.

So, there was always Plan B for me to act on.

"Well, um... Daddy," I fluttered my eyelashes, feeling horribly awkward for even using that wording. "I was hoping you could help me out with that."

He looked my way. There was some fire in his eyes. "So you're expecting special treatment, aren't you?"

"Mom wants us to get along and be friendly and all that good stuff, right? We don't need to have this grade getting in between us."

"Do you expect me to just change your grade?"

"Just use an overly liberal interpretation of my answers."

"You really can't do that with mathematics, Alyssa."

"Then, um..." I blushed. Was he really going to stick to his hard-ass guns?

He let out a long, deep sigh. He stood up, and walked to his classroom door. He closed it, and right after, locked it. It was a curious move to me.

"What's up?" I asked.

His steps were slow, but deliberate. Soon, he was looming right over me, staring down at me, his gaze heavy. "You want to call me Daddy, huh? And expect me to take care of you for that?"

"Um... uh... you said you wanted to take care of both me and my mother, didn't you?"

"I did say that. But all the same, I'm not really a Daddy, am I?"

"Uhm... I guess you're technically not my stepfather until you have the marriage certificate?"

"Yes, but you're not actually my child, are you?"

"Well, no. Unless this is where you reveal something that you've known my mom for eighteen years and nine months?"

He laughed, shaking his head. "No, no. Nothing like that."

Mr. Ford was never this vague with me. He was trying to say something to me. What that was, I had absolutely no clue whatsoever.

Wistfully, he looked away. "No, I don't have any children of my own, and just marrying your mother won't change that. She's a fine woman, but time has ended her reproductive days."

"Well yeah. She always wanted more herself, but things never played out like that." She never said it directly to me, but there was enough for me to infer it. She talked about grandchildren way too much for one thing. The fear of an empty nest was coming at her quick.

"I want more children. She wants more children. Yet no matter how much energy I devote to pleasing her, nothing will come of it. What should we do, Alyssa?"

Why was he asking me this of all things? "I don't know, adopt?"

"We could, yes. But I've always wanted something much more natural."

I shrugged. "Fertility treatments?"

"Throw thousands of dollars down a hole that might not

produce any fruit? I'm fairly sure science hasn't reached the point of reversing menopause anyway."

"I don't know, then."

"Isn't it obvious? There's someone who looks very much like Lisa. Someone who is in the prime of their breeding years, someone who could easily give me the child I desire. That we desire."

He was sort of scaring me with what he was saying. I was trying to come up with an answer to everything he was saying. There was one obvious one, but I was desperately clawing for one that wasn't completely batshit insane.

"You want me to do something immoral to make us family, Alyssa. I think it's only fair that I ask you to do something immoral as well."

Then he made a sudden move to really shock me.

He kissed me.

He kissed me, hard. His hand behind my head, running through my hair, the other going down my back. His tongue pushing in.

Even crazier was the fact that I wasn't fighting him too hard. Maybe I was too paralyzed by shock, but when I started to recover, I just started kissing him back.

I was just as batshit insane as he was, apparently.

The kiss broke, my breath ragged, and I stared at him with wide eyes.

"When we talked about marriage, I made my desire for biological children clear to Lisa. It was the only thing making me second guess my dedication to her. Marriage is about sacrifices, Alyssa. She made a sacrifice to have me, just as I had made sacrifices to have her."

"What... what kind of sacrifices?"

"She would sacrifice her right to have me all to herself, if I could get you to agree to bear my children."

"Bear your children?" I echoed, as if the words he were saying weren't even in English.

"Make your sacrifices too, Alyssa. Your mother has given so much to you. Now it's your time to give to her."

His arms were wrapped so firmly around me, his touch so gentle.

I'd never known so much need as I did at that point. Sure, I was a virgin. Maybe I just didn't understand what it really felt like to have a man touching you like this, holding you like this. I wanted more though. So, so much more.

So it was easy to ignore the insanity of what he was proposing. The weight of what he wanted and what it would mean for me.

All I wanted right now was more of him. A man wanted me badly, and it was a man who I had long secretly lusted for too. It was a perfect storm of making me the irrational little girl that I was. I felt powerless in front of him, he could have asked anything of me and I would have agreed as long as he agreed to keep doing what he was doing.

He hoisted me up, his hands firmly curving around my ass, squeezing me so tightly. His lips wrapped around mine again, and I fully leaned into him, embracing him, relishing the tongue that was pushing through my lips.

I wasn't stopping him. Not one bit.

That was all the permission he needed to keep going. Pushing my shirt up and over my body, his hands were on my bare flesh now.

"You know how long I've been eyeballing you, Alyssa?"

"Mm," I murmured, just enjoying the light, sweet touch he was giving me.

"I see a lot of young teenage girls come into my class. A lot of them are perfectly attractive women. You, though, you sparked something in me. You're truly something unique.

Maybe your eyes made me subconsciously drawn to your mother. I knew you were looking but couldn't touch, but I could touch your mother... and now she's letting me have you."

Swallowing, I tried to consider his words. Was he telling me that he wanted me more than my mother? God, he had a strange way of showing that, yet all the same, fuck, I wasn't complaining either.

Goosebumps were forming all over me. He unhooked my bra, and I felt my breasts fall free of their bonds. He stepped back and gazed upon my bosom. "God, they're so much better than I imagined." He reached for my nipples, rolling them in his fingers. "The right balance of perkiness, puffiness... fuck, why was I born twenty years too soon?"

"You—you're having them now," I murmured.

"I guess I am, but damn, for the longest time I was going to be denied this."

Kissing me down my body, he soon licked the tips of my breasts, little shocks going through me, his hand continuing down my form. Down my sides, across my abdomen, every little hair on my body was standing up in anticipation. He wasted little time in undoing my pants button, those deft fingers of his sliding into my jeans, and over my panties.

"God, you're already dripping wet for me, aren't you? You've been hot for teacher a long time, huh?"

"Uh huh," I said, accompanying it with a weak nod.

"You've wanted me to be bad and take advantage of you for a long time, haven't you?"

Again, I nodded with a whimper.

He kept pressing his naughty assault, worming his way into my panties, pressing on my sex, flesh against flesh, caressing it and causing me to gasp out loud. He pushed deeper, his finger invading my sex, the pressure, the intensity, the thrill of having him there growing so strong.

"Wait, you're still a virgin?"

I swallowed, and then I nodded, as if the fact completely embarrassed me.

"I should have guessed with how awkward you were acting. No matter, a girl's first time should be special, something she's never going to forget."

"Trust me, this is already something I'm going to have a whole lot of trouble forgetting."

"Well, my future daughter, I'm going to show you all the joys, all the bliss, everything. You're not going to want to forget one second of me."

I swallowed. "That confident, huh?"

"Taking care of your partner should always be a man's first concern in love. Always remember that, and never fuck a selfish man. Let that be my first bit of fatherly advice."

I never expected to receive parental wisdom when said parent had their finger firmly laid in my snatch, but I was quickly learning my relationship with Mr. Ford... Ian... Daddy? Whatever it was, it was going to be anything but typical.

He massaged me, he cared for me. I could feel myself shudder underneath his hand, the heat that was burning down there soon spreading through my body.

As he touched me, he rubbed my clit, building me up with only an index finger. I imagined how it would feel with his mouth between my legs, how it would feel with his cock throbbing inside me. How it would feel to have him do what he said he was going to do.

Breed me. Make me carry his child.

It was still too insane to think about.

So I didn't think about it. I just enjoyed it.

Letting the bliss take me. Letting him kiss me, him drawing me close. He stripped off my shoes, my jeans, leaving me naked in front of him besides my panties. I knew that those weren't long for the world either.

I reached toward him, yearning to see him bare as I was. To his credit, he helped me along, stripping off that collared shirt. He proved to me that he was just as toned and firm as I suspected he would be. His chest had fine hairs all across it, and his abs and pecs looked, well, more natural than most I'd seen on typical bodybuilders and the like. He wasn't a bodybuilder, he was just naturally sexy. A man with all the potential strength to be one, but one who would rather use his mind instead.

Which really was sexy all in itself.

His body tickled my fingers as I explored him, learning the curvatures of those muscles. Soon my curious hands went lower, and I felt the bulge that was in his pants. A smile from him, and he undid his belt, letting that fall around his feet and showing me the boxer briefs he was wearing underneath. It wasn't remotely subtle how hard he was for me, the fabric of the undergarment looking like it was desperately straining to keep the beast beneath it contained.

Grazing my hand against it, I realized just how hot and hard it really was.

"God, careful, I've wanted you for so damn long that if you pet me too much I'm going to burst too early, and that won't be helpful to our ultimate goal now, would it?"

A good part of me wanted to keep stroking him. Petting him. Maybe hoping that would deter him.

Another part didn't want to derail his plan.

What the heck was wrong with me?

Now with him as naked as I was, he was out to make sure I was more naked than him once again. Two hands grabbed the hem of my panties, and he jerked them right down my legs, and I did little to stop him. In fact, I was closing my legs just long enough to help him.

Was I really turning into my teacher's slut? Daddy's slut?

He laid his flat hand across my chest, pushing me down

flat across his desk. My legs parted for him, his kisses quickly going lower across my flesh.

I damn near came when I realized his true intentions. A single powerful kiss on my nub and lightning shot through me. He didn't stop there, his machinations so driven and sending shivers through me again and again.

His tongue carving his name in my sex, I grabbed handfuls of his hair, coping with the rising tide inside of me. He wasn't shaken by my irrational yanks, only pushing himself further to please me, his hands wandering my body and giving each and every bit of me the attention it so richly deserved. Handfuls of my ass, my sides, fingerfucking me, kneading my breasts, Ian was completely aware that there were other things to make me feel so desired beyond just my slit and my nub.

That he even found the latter there was miles more than I expected of boys who were my own age.

Even between my legs, he was in complete control of me. My back arching, I was writhing against him, aching with incredible need for him. I was moaning for him, almost in rhythm to his tongue fucking me.

Legs closing around him, I fought against my own pleasure, wanting to drag this out as much as I possibly could. Christ, if he could eat pussy like this, it was no wonder to me why Mom was so willing to make concessions like this.

He looked up at me, seeing that I was gritting my teeth, bracing myself. That apparently was a no-no because he increased his intensity.

My young, virginal body couldn't really cope with something like this. This was a man with decades of experience compared to my complete lack thereof. It was an easy win for him.

The tide hit me so strongly so suddenly, and I screamed out so loudly. I was worried if anyone would hear us, but I comforted myself that a man like Ian Ford wouldn't take such a wanton risk if there was a chance of us being caught.

Bliss rushing through me along with adrenaline, a smile curled wider on my face. There were so many taboos with what I was doing here. My teacher, my soon-to-be stepfather, my first time, my mother's future husband, the fact that he wanted to do far more than fuck me.

It was wild. I tried not to think about it too much and just enjoyed what was coming my way.

Covered in cold sweat, I watched as Ian rose up. He hooked his hands in his boxers and pushed them down, his cock springing forward. For the first time I was faced with the daunting realization that he wanted to put that thing in me.

All of its throbbing nature. I was briefly at a loss of how logistics for all of this would possibly work. That thing entering me? Was that a thing that was supposed to happen?

As daunting as it was, I took a deep breath and cleared my head of it.

My teacher was looking down at me, his desire so clear. I was waiting for him to come forward, thrust himself inside me with wild abandon, with no care given to my lack of experience.

No, he was going to do something far worse.

He was going to tease me.

"Tell me you want this, Alyssa." His cock lingered outside of my slit, throbbing on top of it.

"Um..."

"Tell me you want this. Tell me you want me to fuck you."

"I... I..." What did he expect me to do right now? My hormones were fully in control. On some level I knew this was a bad idea, that this was completely insane. Yet I wasn't going to stop him. Not in a million years.

"I want to hear it from your lips. There's no going back

from what I'm going to do to you, Alyssa. I want you to understand that."

Nodding, I took a deep breath. "I want you," I said, barely above a whisper.

"Clearer."

"I want you to fuck me."

"Who do you want to fuck you?"

"I want you to fuck me, Mr. Ford."

"No, not that. This isn't something between student and teacher, Alyssa."

I raised an eyebrow. "I want you to fuck me, Ian?"

"You know what this is. Tell me exactly what you want."

It would be bad enough if he were teasing me with his words. All while he spoke though he rubbed his cock against me, tickling my nub. Together they were quite the cruel tease.

"Who am I?"

"My step-dad?"

"What do you want me to do?"

"Fuck me."

"Say it."

My heart was racing. I never thought such a lewd phrase would cross my lips unironically.

I couldn't resist him. Not one bit.

"Fuck me, Daddy. Please, fuck me."

There was a sick twisted smile on his face. You never know what a person truly desires, but damn if I never expected this out of Mr. Ford.

"With pleasure, little girl," he said, his cock sliding off my nub and pressing into my slit.

To my surprise, he didn't just impale me on himself. He took me on slowly, pressing against my purity as he prepared to take it from me in the least pure way possible.

In a flash, he leaned over, kissed me on the lips, held my hands in his, and pushed himself in.

A clusterfuck of sensations, I barely noticed anything like pain. No, instead I was fully consumed by him.

Fully consumed by Daddy.

Holding me down, our tongues entwining, his body against mine, he took his time letting my body adjust to his throbbing invader.

"You're mine now. Mine to hold. Mine to protect. Mine to fuck," he whispered into my ear, his words so intense on top of everything else.

He didn't waste much time in just savoring the moment. He soon started to fuck me properly. Slowly at first, but he didn't linger on that timid pace for that long. He was all the way inside me, filling me to the brim with himself.

It was an endless assault of powerful waves crashing through my body. I moaned just a little bit louder with every penetration, our bodies wet and rubbing against one another, our passion only growing.

Murmuring for him, he took me faster, he took me harder.

He took me deeper. His arms hooked under my knees folding me up like I was an accordion. His little fuck ball, he used the leverage to take me deeper, harder.

I wasn't going to last long. I couldn't dream of resisting like he had. He was introducing me to so many new things. Nibbling on my lip I found myself grinding against him, only wanting more like the little slut I was doomed to become.

My fingers clawed down his back, so fierce that I was sure that I was going to leave a mark on him. I couldn't help it. I was already shaking. Just from those rapid thrusts of his, I was close.

All I could do was hold on tight and desperately try to ride out this wonderful storm.

When it erupted, it consumed me. Coming out from my core, all of it shot out in every which way, all through my body. Everything ached with bliss, and yet...

He didn't stop. Daddy was hardly done yet. He was torturing me, pushing me further, still fucking me like the maniac he was.

"I can't fucking get enough of you. Years of pent up need for you, Alyssa. I'm not going to rush through my first taste so easily. I'm going to savor it to the fullest."

Breathing heavily, I nodded. There were no questions, I just wanted more of whatever he was offering.

"Bend over the desk. I'm going to take you like the daughter-slut you are."

Swallowing, I obeyed as he let me up, withdrawing himself from me. I obeyed him, bracing myself on his desk.

He didn't hesitate, thrusting himself into me from behind. I cried out and almost came again from that alone.

This time he was coming at me even harder, even faster. I soon found myself bucking into him, the echoes of our colliding flesh bouncing through the room.

His hands were firmly on my hips, allowing him to rock me harder with every thrust. Every penetration. I was already leaning back into him, and he was swift to take me into his hands, holding me against him as he fucked the daylights out of me.

My vision was a blurry mess, and I called out just a bit louder when he put his fingers between my legs, and rubbed my clit perfectly in tune with his fucking.

All of me was shaking, all of me hurting so wonderfully. Pinned against him, I can feel his desperation too, the need he had, and I instinctively knew that he was close.

"Tell me," he whispered in a way that I could hear in spite of myself.

"What?"

"Tell me what you want me to do. Daddy is buried deep inside you, ready to fill you. But you have to tell me you want it."

He was waiting for my permission. Putting me on the spot.

I didn't care. I knew what he wanted, and I was going to give it to him swiftly and without waiting one moment.

"Fuck me, Daddy. Fill me, Daddy," I let out between moans. "Fuck your little girl! Knock her up! Please, Daddy!"

"I'm never going to let you down, Alyssa," he whispered into my ears, that being the last thing he needed to push him over the edge.

His grip on me only tightened, and one last stroke of his cock inside me, and one last rub of my button, and I was screaming for him.

It was so much more intense than anything else I had experienced by his hand yet. I was shaking, trembling, I needed more words to describe how I felt. How intense it was... how GOOD it was.

Daddy had ruined me, not by taking my virginity, but by making it so no other man could ever compete with him.

Holding me close, he quivered inside me. All of that lust, that need, that desire of his was roaring out of him with a powerful groan. Feeling that warmth lash out, flood me.

Knowing what it was. What I was risking. Who was doing it to me.

Every taboo I broke though only made the feeling sweeter.

Who knew it didn't take much to turn me into an incest slut?

My heart pounding, Daddy held me close. I laid flat on his desk, and he was on top of me. It was oddly comfortable, and comforting for that matter.

Nothing lasts forever, though. Soon he had to pull himself

away from me, and the sinful evidence of our tryst began to leak out from my body. He tried to push some of it back in, but gravity wasn't going to let that much stay inside of me.

I could barely move without feeling the ache of what I had done. I never knew something that might be akin to pain could feel so damn good.

Daddy sat on the desk beside me, still naked. That was what he was now. The uncertainty was gone. He wasn't my teacher anymore, and he was never just Ian. He was Daddy, something I never thought I would have, and something I definitely never thought I would have like this.

He was looking my way, up and down my tired, sweaty naked body.

"God, I was doubting that I would be able to keep myself strong enough to take care of the needs of two women at once, but looking at you, I can already feel my cock twitching. It's not going to be an issue at all."

I let out a sigh, still way too much in shock to truly say anything.

"Take your time. There's no rush. I'll take you out for dinner after we get ourselves together. After all, you need your strength."

My bottom lip trembled. "What, for the baby?" I still was shocked that I didn't even fight that. My hormonal self was just all too consumed with need for him.

"Well, I suppose." He rubbed his chin. "But I was more concerned with keeping you healthy so I can fuck the shit out of you again."

"If you say so, Daddy." I smirked at the ridiculousness of it. It was obscene. Wrong. Taboo. Whatever. It didn't matter.

All that did matter? Is that it was mine.

And I wouldn't have it any other way.

THE END
Get Access to over 20 more FREE Erotica Downloads at Shameless Book Deals

SHAMELESS BOOK DEALS is a website that shamelessly brings you the very best erotica at the best prices from the best authors to your inbox every day. Sign up to our newsletter to get access to the daily deals and the Shameless Free Story Archive!

AFTER HOURS - CORDOVA SKYE

When I took a break after my first semester of college, I thought it would be a free ride courtesy of the wealthy new man of the house. Roland King didn't believe in avoiding adult responsibilities, though, and soon after my arrival home I was working 9 to 5 in his office.

Before I knew it, I was staying late with this dominant older man, and our taboo after hours fun was going to make me a woman...with the baby bump to prove it.

It only took me one month of college to realize that college *sucked*. No more coasting through the subjects I'd breezed through in high school; no more teachers who'd known me for four years and looked the other way because I was a "good girl." Sure, college was a chance to reinvent myself, but it was also so much work that I never had time for friends or parties, and I - who had always thought I liked school - discovered I hated it when I couldn't effortlessly be the smartest girl in class.

Unfortunately, my mother had taken me moving away to school as an opportunity to get re-married, so she wasn't around to listen to my tearful stories about how horrible it all was. I didn't get a chance to move back home until the semester was over, and when I did finally get to pack up and escape, it wasn't home to the two-story house I'd grown up in. It was into the sprawling estate owned by mom's new husband, Roland King.

I expected our new wealth to work in my favor. After all, if a girl can't be spoiled because her mom managed to hook a millionaire, what does it take, right? I'd wanted to shed the image of sweet little Didi while I was at college, but now I daydreamed of lounging on private beaches and visiting exotic lands, and the parties I imagined weren't frat house keggers but social events. I spent the plane trip home reading fashion magazines and happily daydreaming of myself in those skimpy, sexy designer clothes, sipping fine wine and seducing every man I met.

Those daydreams lasted all the way up until I met Roland King himself.

My new stepfather was intimidating, tall and broad-shouldered, stiff-backed like he'd been in the military, with intense dark eyes. I knew he was in his fifties, but the only sign of age was a touch of gray at the temples of his neatly trimmed hair; his face was smooth and unlined, and god help me, he was *hot*. I found myself standing up straighter when I met him, and as he looked me over I was all too aware of how my suddenly improved posture made my breasts stick out from my chest.

My instinct was to cross my arms over my chest and hide myself. That's what good Didi, high school Didi, had always done. But I was going to be socialite Candace now, so I forced my hands behind my back and tried not to blush when I realized that just made my chest more prominent.

"So, you're Candace." Roland's voice was rich and commanding; he was obviously a man used to getting whatever he wanted. "Your mother tells me you had some difficulty at school this term."

"Yes, sir." I put on the pleading look that always got me sympathy from my mother. "I had a terrible course load, and I was really burnt out by the end of the semester. I was afraid I wasn't going to pass." I smiled at him. "I'm so glad to be home so I can recover."

"I hope you have some plans of what to do with yourself."

"Well, I guess I'd like to travel, but it's winter and…"

He waved me to silence. "Not frivolities. You're a grown woman; you need something worthwhile to fill your time. You must have some idea of what sort of work you'd like to do."

"Work?" I asked, as if I'd never heard the word before. "But you…" I choked off the words. Reminding him he was rich was just going to make it sound like Mom was a gold digger. "I mean, I need time off. For my mental and emotional health."

He was shaking his head, unimpressed by my argument. "You need to develop some backbone, young lady. Grow up and learn to deal with the world. I'll give you a month to find a job, but you'd better believe I'll know if you aren't really looking."

Or else what? I wondered angrily. I hated the domineering tone he was taking with me…but at the same time, there was something really hot about how naturally he assumed he was in charge. I could see why my mom had fallen right into bed with him, and that made me even angrier.

I took a deep breath, careful not to let my temper get the better of me. "And if I can't find a job?" I asked, trying to sound reasonable, if not actually obedient. "It's a tough market out there."

"Don't worry, there are always internships open at my office." He smiled, confident that he'd won this round. "Unpaid, of course. So I suggest you take your job search seriously."

"How generous of you," I said, forcing a smile.

"I can be very generous, Candace," he said, looking me up and down, "to people who deserve it."

I excused myself to go see my mother and left his office. Fury burned in my veins at how he was ruining my daydreams, but it wasn't just anger that made heat rush through me. I couldn't get his deep, commanding voice out of my head, or stop thinking about the way he'd looked at me. Had it been my imagination that his gaze had lingered on my chest? *Undressing me with his eyes* was a phrase I'd only seen in romances, but after the way Roland had looked at me, I thought I understood what it meant.

Hours later, as I climbed into a strange bed in a strange room that I couldn't quite think of as mine. I was still turning it all over in my mind. Roland King was a man used to being in charge - of himself and of other people. What would it take to break that self-control? Could *I* do it? I knew I shouldn't try; he was my stepfather, now, and I'd be betraying my mother. It was wrong on every level possible, and yet once the fantasy started playing out I couldn't erase it from my mind.

I slid a finger down between my legs, fondling myself, a thrill of excitement running through me as I pictured him claiming me for his own. I was still a virgin; would he be gentle with me when he took my innocence? Or... A tremor ran down my spine and I rubbed harder around my clit as my hot juices soaked my lower lips. Would he just take me, hard and raw, and call it a fitting lesson for my taboo desires?

My free hand pressed hard against my mouth, muffling my moans as I came. It was the most intense orgasm I'd ever had, and I felt guilty that I'd gotten myself off the to image of my stepfather bending me over a desk and fucking me.

Guilt wasn't enough to make my forbidden fantasy go away, however, and as I fell asleep I was picturing just how I'd get Roland's attention.

~

I DID LOOK for a job over the next few weeks; I believed Roland when he said he'd know if I was lying to him. I also did a lot of shopping, though most of what I bought wasn't what you'd call office appropriate. It wasn't anything sweet little Didi ever would have considered wearing, either, but if my new step-daddy wanted me to grow up, I'd show him just how much of a woman I could be.

Mom was glad to see me showing more interest in my appearance, which made me feel guiltier about my plans than the idea of seducing Roland did. But, I reasoned, all I planned to do was give him opportunity; I certainly wasn't responsible for what happened if I offered up a little temptation. And if he did give in to temptation, I was sure he'd be as eager to keep it quiet as I was. What kind of man would want it to get out that he'd fucked his nineteen-year-old step-daughter?

Besides, all that rationalization went right out the window when Roland called me into his office, four weeks to the day after he'd first ordered me to get a job.

"You're looking well, Candace," he said as I entered.

I hadn't dressed provocatively for the meeting, but I was all in winter white that set off my peaches-and-cream complexion and made my hair look like polished gold, and I had the satisfaction of watching his eyes as they lingered on the way my tight sweater outlined my breasts and then moved slowly down my body.

"Thank you, Daddy," I said sweetly, smoothing my skirt to draw attention to how the soft fabric hugged my hips. "Mama took me shopping."

He frowned slightly, though I couldn't tell if it was because of my familiarity, the deliberately childish terms I'd chosen, or the fact that Mom had taken me out for a whole new wardrobe. Whichever it was, I was glad to get a reaction out of him, a break in his stern facade.

"My people tell me you still don't have a job." His eyes rose to meet mine, but then dropped right back to my chest. "You realize what that means, of course."

"Isn't there anything I can do to make you reconsider?" I asked. If I'd had any experience outside of my bedtime fantasies, I would have tried to seduce him right there, but I suspected any attempt I made would come off as ridiculous, or worse, he'd realize what I was doing and I'd be out of luck before I even got started pushing his buttons.

My fantasies weren't about him just giving in, anyway. That felt dirty and cheap. No, I wanted to push him until he bent me over and gave me the lesson I so obviously deserved.

"Your mother's been too soft on you, girl," he said, shaking his head. "It's time you learned to work for what you want." He finally took his eyes off me, glancing down as he typed something into his computer. The printer at the end of his desk hummed softly and spit out a sheet of paper, which he handed to me. "Starting Monday, you'll be working directly under me. I'll make a proper woman out of you."

I murmured thanks, my hand shaking slightly as I took the paper from him, and hoped I wasn't blushing as I bolted from the office. My heart pounded and heat burned under my skin.

Make a woman out of me. I hoped Roland hadn't guessed how much I hoped he'd do exactly that.

∽

WORKING for Roland wasn't bad, really, but over the first few days I discovered it was very *frustrating*. Roland was kind of a hard-ass, but when I wasn't the one getting ordered around, watching him take charge of things was pretty hot. It didn't take me long to figure out which employees were likely to be the targets of his attention, and whenever I could I hung out near them, just so I could hear his voice and watch him while he gave orders.

Those first few days, I tried to behave, but by the end of my first week my sexual frustration combined with my reluctance to work and I hatched a plan. He couldn't fire me, I reasoned; my mom would never let him kick me out, and he'd insisted that as long as I was living with them, I had to have a job. And I'd wanted to see how far I could push that steely resolve almost from the moment I met him. Being too much of a flirt around home would have alerted my mother that something was going on, but at work she'd never know, and I wouldn't *really* have to worry about pushing Roland too far and having one of my naughtier daydreams come true.

I wasn't sure if that was a relief or a disappointment, but it meant I was free to do something outrageous.

The next Monday, I showed up at work in a virginal pink sweater, which I promptly removed to show off the sheer, low-cut white blouse beneath. Roland didn't say anything, but every time I moved, every time I leaned over or reached for something, he noticed. Him, and every other man in the office. I reveled in the attention even while I pretended not to notice, playing the role of the sweet, helpful intern to the hilt.

When I shrugged back into my sweater to go home, Roland still couldn't take his eyes off my chest. I spent the drive home with my pulse pounding; I didn't think I could keep this up if he confronted me about it, but part of me wished he'd act on my blatant invitation.

Unfortunately, we made it home without him laying a hand on me, or even saying anything. I caught him looking at me all through dinner, though, and when I could escape up to my room I immediately took a shower, my fingers buried in my aching pussy while the water pounded down on me.

After the success of the first day, my little game got easier and harder. I liked the attention I got from the men, and I loved knowing that Roland couldn't keep his eyes off me as my necklines got lower and my skirts got shorter. I even kind of liked knowing that the women in the office were complaining about me behind my back; it felt like a success marker of being younger and hotter than any of them. Not being able to flirt back was hard, though; I'd never realized how stifling being sweet little Didi was. It felt like I was always turned on by the feeling of male eyes on me, a subliminal tension in the air that made my smiles a little friendlier and my laughter a little brighter.

Then I finally crossed a line and Roland couldn't ignore my behavior any more.

It was late Friday afternoon, and I'd just brought coffee in to one of the conference rooms. The three men using it were among my biggest admirers, and knowing they were looking at me - sometimes covertly, sometimes blatantly - always distracted me. My hands shook a little as I served them, a combination of the shivery adrenaline rush from their attention, the warmth in my belly and the low, steady throb between my legs that I knew I was going to have to deal with after work. I was blushing as much from the thoughts in my mind as from their lavish compliments, and my head was full of things I wished I could say in return.

I fumbled one of the cups of coffee and spilled it all down my chest, staining my white blouse and soaking it to translucence.

"Oh my gosh, I'm so sorry!" I said, flushing partially from genuine embarrassment at their laughter, and partly because I knew they could see the outline of my nipples through the thin lace of my bra.

"You should be," one of the men said, leering at my chest. "That's a waste of good coffee."

Before I could stop myself, I stood a little straighter, chest thrust toward him. "Well, it doesn't have to go to waste."

Silence greeted my words, followed by the sharp, damning crack of Roland's voice from behind me. I almost died on the spot; I hadn't realized he was coming to this meeting, or that he'd followed me into the room.

"Candace. My office, now. Gentlemen, this meeting will have to take place Monday."

I bit my lip, covering my chest as I turned around. Roland looked furious, and my heart did a little flip-flop that had nothing to do with fear. I couldn't remember him looking sexier, even when he'd originally laid down the law about this job.

I scuttled past him, out of the conference room, keeping my head down. In the room beyond I could hear whispers as people undoubtedly speculated about my fate. I wondered anxiously if Roland really would fire me, kick me out, make me manage on my own when that was exactly what I'd been trying to avoid.

Suddenly, all of the games I'd been playing, confident I was untouchable, seemed like a terrible idea.

The sound of the door shutting - not slammed, but a firm

and deliberate *click* - made me start crying. "I'm sorry," I said, and in that moment I really meant it. "Please don't fire me."

"I almost believe you," he said dryly, walking around me to his desk. He settled back in the massive leather chair, watching me over steepled fingers. "What *am* I going to do with you, Candace? I've brought you into my business, taken you under my wing, done everything in my power to show you the path to success in this world...and this is the thanks I get." He flicked the fingers of one hand toward me. "Stand up straight when I talk to you, girl. Don't slouch."

Reluctantly, I straightened, letting my arms drop to my sides. In spite of my embarrassment, my nipples still strained against the cold, wet fabric covering my chest.

"I hoped, when I married your mother, that I'd get an heir with some ambition," he continued. "But you don't have that kind of ambition, do you, Candace?"

His voice was pure torture, the rich tones reaching out to stroke over my clit. I shifted where I stood, squeezing my thighs together. "No, sir. Not really."

He nodded; I couldn't read anything in his expression. "Then we'll have to deal with this a different way. Since you can't behave like a professional and get your work done during the day, you'll be staying late with me for the foreseeable future. And coming in on the weekends."

"But that's not fair!" I exclaimed. "I barely have any free time as it is!"

"And," Roland continued mercilessly, "since you can't seem to keep from distracting the *working* members of my team, beginning tomorrow your desk will be in this office, where I can supervise you. Go get your things. Now."

I stamped my foot and turned, not caring that my short skirt flipped up and gave him a flash of my ass. Roland didn't call me back or say anything; I thought maybe he hadn't noticed.

He certainly couldn't miss how long it took me to gather my few personal belongings from my desk, because while I was doing it, everyone filtered out of the office, even the people who usually lingered to wrap up a few things before the weekend. The whole place was dead silent when I carried the small box of knick-knacks and files into Roland's private office and asked, "Where should I put this?"

"Set it in the corner," he said, and while I obeyed he once again shut the door, locking it behind me.

"I feel I have been extremely patient with you, Candace," he said calmly as he walked back toward his desk. "In spite of your rather childish acting out with my employees."

"Yes, sir," I said sullenly. He wasn't wrong, but I was too angry - and frustrated - to admit it. I felt like I was buzzing with pent-up *something*, and his voice - deep and smooth and utterly, annoyingly calm - just twisted the tension inside my body tighter.

"I intended to teach you the necessary lessons of being an adult in the workplace," he continued, "but it seems you require more…hands-on instruction. And perhaps, something to force you to be responsible."

I felt a little burst of fear under my annoyance. Was he going to kick me out? Teach me responsibility by making me take care of myself? I licked my lips, realizing just how spoiled I really was, in spite of the hours I spent working at the office. I knew if I had to get a job on my own, it wouldn't be nearly so lenient as this one.

"I'm sorry," I said, and meant it, even if I was only sorry I'd gotten myself onto such thin ice.

"I'm sure you are," Roland said dryly, "but a half-hearted apology is not going to change my mind, I'm afraid."

"What…what are you going to do to me?" I asked in a tiny voice.

Roland stepped closer, and I was struck again by how tall

and fit he was, how sexy for all that he was old enough to be my father...*was* my father, by marriage at least. His big hands cupped my face, warm and strong, and heat shivered through me at the intensity of his gaze. "I told you, Candace. I'm going to teach you how to be a woman instead of a spoiled little girl."

My breath caught in my throat. He couldn't mean...he could not *possibly* be saying...

He leaned down, hands holding me in place while his lips covered mine in a kiss that made my trapped breath escape in a moan. The heat coiled in my stomach spread through my body like wildfire, flushing my skin, throbbing between my legs. I could feel my panties growing damp, and suddenly the short skirt I'd flaunted all day felt too short, left me feeling exposed and unprotected. All he had to do was reach down, and there would be nothing at all between his fingers and the damp lace that barely covered my throbbing cunt.

I moaned again, shivering while his lips gently forced mine open and his tongue invaded my mouth. My hands clutched at his arms, wrinkling the immaculate lines of his suit, but neither of us noticed or cared.

By the time Roland released me, I was breathing heavily, my nipples contracted into such hard, obscene nubs against my shirt that he couldn't fail to notice them, any more than he could fail to notice the way I shifted my weight in an effort to ease the demanding ache of my pussy.

Roland put an arm's length between us, and as he stepped back I briefly wondered if *this* was my punishment, getting me all hot and bothered and then walking away and expecting me to act like nothing was wrong. If it was, I didn't see any way I could manage to behave; my whole body was on fire, and I wanted desperately to touch myself and release the overwhelming need he'd triggered.

Luckily, Roland wasn't that cruel.

"Now, Candace," he said, his eyes sweeping over me, taking in my flushed face and the way my breasts rose and fell with my quickened breathing, "do you think that is a lesson you're ready to learn."

"Yes," I said, barely able to get the word out. I knew I'd be humiliated if he was just toying with me, but I couldn't even entertain the idea of trying to play coy and say no. Not when I desperately wanted his hands back on me, wanted him to teach me everything an experienced older man would know. "I want to learn. I want you to teach me how to be a woman."

He smiled, the expression just a little mocking, and caught my wrist to pull me in against him. His free hand slid down to cup my ass. "Daddy isn't mad, Didi," he said, using my nickname for the first time. He squeezed my ass cheek. "But Daddy wants to make sure this is a lesson you don't forget."

The hand squeezing my ass slapped me sharply, and I lurched forward against him with a little squeal. Roland chuckled and led me to his desk; while I'd been cleaning my desk out, he'd been clearing the top of his, so there was a gleaming expanse of bare wood instead of his usual papers and computer.

He turned me around and boosted me up on it, just like I was a little girl sitting on a counter. My skirt rode up and left my ass nearly bare on the wood, just my panties in the way… and then Roland's hands slid up my thighs, his thumbs caressing the damp fabric that covered my aching cunt.

His light touch sent another burst of heat through me and I squirmed in place, so distracted that I almost missed his question. "Tell me, Didi, are you a virgin?"

The flush in my face turned into the heat of embarrassment, and I wasn't sure if it was because he'd asked, or because the answer was yes. I nodded, unable to look him in the eyes, and felt his fingers hook into the waistband of my panties.

"Your mother implied as much," he said with satisfaction, "but she's not always terribly aware of what's going on around her. She's the type who needs to be sheltered, Didi, and protected. You," and he tugged my panties down, sliding them over my hips, "are made for greater things."

I shifted so he could pull my panties down my legs, leaving me completely bare down there. My breath came faster; I could smell my own lust in the air, and I knew he could smell how much I wanted him.

Before I knew what he was doing, he tipped me back, so I had to support myself on my elbows, and spread my legs. He leaned down, burying his face against my cunt, tongue sliding hot and demanding between my lower lips. I cried out, surprise and raw pleasure crashing over me, my whole body jerking as if he'd just struck me with lightning.

"Delicious," he proclaimed when he raised his head. "I believe this lesson will be a pleasure for us both."

I nodded, unable to form words, my whole body wound tight and shaking. After all my weeks of trying to break Roland's reserve, my success shocked me; I don't think I'd ever really believed I could do it, that this was possible. I couldn't be dreaming, though; I'd never felt like this, never even imagined I *could* feel like this.

Roland licked his lips and leaned down to kiss me again. I could taste myself on him, salt and musk, and I wondered if he'd go down on me again, if he expected me to go down on *him*...

The sensation of a finger penetrating my virgin pussy sent all such thoughts out of my mind. I gasped, hips jerking so hard I would have slid off the desk if Roland's own body hadn't held me in place. Roland's hands were like the rest of him, refined, yet large and masculine, and his touch was stronger and more demanding than my own. I whimpered, my pussy clenching down around him, both shocked by the intruder stretching my tender flesh, and eager, *desperate*, for more.

And Roland had more to give. While the fingers of one hand fucked my pussy, his other hand tugged his belt free and unfastened the expensive slacks he wore. I stared down along my body, eager to see him for the first time, and my pussy gave another tight spasm around his fingers when he freed his cock.

He was huge. I'd known he would be; there was nothing small about my stepfather. But that still didn't prepare me for the long, thick, dark-flushed shaft that curved up from between his legs.

"Roland…" His cock looked like it would stretch me wide and fill me all the way, and I didn't know how I'd ever take it, but I wanted it. Even the idea that I could get pregnant, that his huge shaft looked like it could shoot his seed directly into my womb, didn't deter me. Having Roland's baby would be worth it.

"You're not on the pill, are you?" Roland asked, as if he could read my mind.

"No," I breathed.

He pulled his fingers out of me with an obscene sound. "Then I sincerely hope your lesson in responsibility will bear fruit," he said.

His hands closed on my hips, pulling me a little closer to the edge of the desk. I lay back on the smooth wood, my legs instinctively wrapping around his hips as he pressed into me. I moaned, tipping my head back as I stretched around him, wider than I'd ever dreamed. I was so wet that he had no trouble filling me, his cock sliding deeper and deeper until I felt like there was no part of me that wasn't wrapped tight around him.

I'd never felt anything so amazing. I cried out with utter abandon, oblivious to everything but his body thrusting and grinding against mine, the sound of his rough breathing, the slap of his balls against my ass every time he plunged deep inside my virgin cunt. My hands grabbed at the slick wood of the desk, seeking leverage to push back against him, and my legs clung to him in a desperate effort to drag him impossibly deeper inside me.

With my legs anchored around his hips, his hands were free to play with my tits. The buttons on my flimsy blouse gave way as he pulled it open; the front clasp of my bra yielded to a twist of his fingers. The lace slipped away and my breasts bounced free, bobbing with each driving thrust.

Roland's hands curved over the tender mounds, kneading and pinching, tweaking the already hard nipples until I cried out. Too much, too many sensations, my wide-stretched cunt and my tight, aching nipples, the rough handling of my breasts...and then Roland's mouth closed over my right nipple, sucking, and I lost myself completely, my orgasm crashing over me in a wave.

I wailed, my whole body tightening with raw, primal pleasure. I could feel his cock, throbbing and pulsing as my cunt squeezed tight, milking him until the hot jet of his seed shot deep into my unprotected womb. It filled me until I could feel the thick, sticky heat of him slipping from my pussy, confirmation of my irrevocable step into womanhood.

Anxiety pushed its way through the warm, comfortable lassitude that followed such an intense orgasm. "I could be pregnant," I thought, and didn't realize I'd said the words aloud until Roland answered.

"If not tonight, then soon," he said, stroking my cheek. "Motherhood is a fine lesson in responsibility. And I do so look forward to watching you grow up, my Didi."

I stared at him, turning the idea over in my mind. I

wondered how we'd explain to my mother, but I knew Roland would think of something; he didn't want to hurt her any more than I did.

And I *did* want him to keep teaching me lessons just like this one.

"Can you make sure I've got the lesson right, Daddy?" I asked, wrapping my arms around him.

He smiled, and I knew we'd keep working after hours as long as it took to make my belly swell with his child.

THE END
Get Access to over 20 more FREE Erotica Downloads at Shameless Book Deals

SHAMELESS BOOK DEALS is a website that shamelessly brings you the very best erotica at the best prices from the best authors to your inbox every day. Sign up to our newsletter to get access to the daily deals and the Shameless Free Story Archive!

FIRST TIME FOR THE MAN OF THE HOUSE - CANDY QUINN

When the man of the house checked us into our hotel as man and wife, I just laughed it off.

But when things started getting steamy on the beach, I couldn't help but unleash all my most forbidden fantasies. Even when another couple stops to watch, I can't deny him anything.

And when he finally takes me on our 'marital' bed, I know he's right.

I'm all his.

Girls aren't supposed to want to fuck their daddies, even their step-daddies, but what can I say? I've got a rebel streak. Besides, daddies aren't supposed to want to fuck their girls either, but I caught him staring at me with the biggest hard-on I've ever seen in my life.

You see, we were on the beach, sandwiched between the ocean and a pool. It's just been the two of us for so long now, we're just comfortable hanging out together.

I had my headset on, listening to my latest favs as I danced at the edge of the pool. It was a warm, late summer day, and I only had on my bikini. And admittedly, it was skimpy and a bit tiny, even for a bikini. I'd bought it with permission just before my breasts hit their peak, and so the tiny little triangles of fabric barely kept my nipples covered, let alone any of my tits themselves.

I wasn't thinking about how I looked like that, long blonde hair flowing about my bare shoulders, breasts jiggling with my motion. My rather large, bubbly butt on full display as the cheeks swallowed up the tiny little thread of my thong.

But still when one song ended, and another was about to play, I broke my rhythm and concentration and fluttered my eyes open. Only to be greeted by such a shocking... marvelous sight.

He had been with me all along, reading on his tablet. Except now it was put aside, and he was watching me.

I could just gush endlessly about his cock, which I got to see poking out of his shorts. I mean, that's how it was when at full mast. But even putting aside that thick, veiny daddy dick, he was just a ruggedly handsome, stunning man. Sure, he had a bit of silver in his hair, but that just made him foxier. He was six foot four, with broad shoulders, thick biceps, veiny forearms and abs to die for. And he never skipped leg day either, with gorgeous calves and powerful thighs.

So you see, he's the whole package. Topped off with a chiseled jaw, intense blue eyes, and the handsomest smile.

And I guess I always knew that. I mean, my friends would come over and gush about how hot he was. I swear, sometimes I'd get jealous, thinking they wanted to fuck him more than they wanted to hang out with me.

But it wasn't just that. No, I was also jealous because if they wanted to, and he wanted to, they could do just that. They could screw and no one would bat an eye at an eighteen year old girl throwing herself at an older, successful, sexy man. And I wasn't allowed. Even when I expressed agreement with my friends that he was hot, they'd give me this grossed out expression and I'd have to say that I was just joking.

I slid my sunglasses up over my eyes, wondering if he'd caught me staring. It felt like I'd been staring for an eternity, but I guess it was only a few seconds. A few twitches of his cock to the rhythm of his heart. Between my thighs, I grew warm, and I wondered if I should dart upstairs and hide in my room with my vibrator and the vivid memory of his throbbing dick and wandering eyes.

Instead, I started to dance again, this time with all the awareness that he was watching. Before, I'd simply been mindlessly moving to the rhythm of the beat, letting my body do as it wanted. Now that I knew he wanted a show, I figured I'd give him one.

I've always been a naughty girl. He got me a laptop when I was a girl, and now that I'm an adult, it's filled to the brim with porn. Movies, erotic eBooks, gifs, sexy photoshoots... I liked it all. But I especially liked it when the girl cried out, "Oh Daddy!" and I could fantasize that she was me.

My hand ran up my ass as I bumped my hips to the side, my full lips parted as I pretended to mouth the words. My tongue ran across the seam as I looked to the side, glancing to see if he was still watching me.

And oh, he was. Those intense eyes of his were glued to me and my every movement. I could feel them roaming over me, from head to toe. Watching me slide my hand over my ass, wishing it was his much bigger palm.

It was obvious in retrospect I guess. We were always so close and open. I never shied from talking about sex stuff with him, and he was always open and frank, though never pervy. And when I graduated high school, he promised me I always have a place here with him, encouraged me to take some time off from school and relax. At home with him. On trips with him.

We'd been like a close, in love couple ever since, and whenever we'd stay at some hotel, we'd be mistaken for just that, again and again. We'd either laugh it off, or... as time went on, we got playful.

He would wink at me, then put his arm around my shoulder, holding me close as the clerk checked us into our room.

"Just got married, taking our honeymoon," he'd said to the one at this very resort. The place so posh, we even had our own pool and segment to the beach. It really did feel like a honeymoon. Minus the sex, that is... which was eating at us both.

And as time went on, that was getting more and more obvious. At least to me. I don't know when exactly we fell over that line of playing around to being serious. Or maybe it's always been serious, and we just didn't want to admit it.

But he was watching me dance with a hard-on that was making my mouth water, and I wasn't going to let the chance go by without showing him how I really feel.

I raised my arms up over my head, in a move that I always tried to resist before.

Why?

Well, I knew that when I raised my hands up, my bikini strings rose up too, and those little triangles that barely concealed me started rising up and up. Finally I could feel that little string hitch on my stiff nipples. The sensation felt so good, and I moaned with excitement as I fluttered my eyes shut. My hips kept wriggling back and forth, and I prayed that my bikini wouldn't be able to resist snapping up the second it finally made it past my nipples, flashing him front on.

Lucky, I didn't have to wait long before that erotic sensation built to a crescendo, and the skimpy top flew up to hit my chin, letting my tits finally be free of its tight constraint.

I was all ready to feign a gasp of shock and look surprised, but before I got to do anything more than gasp, I became aware of my daddy's arms wrapped around me. Those thick, muscular arms, so hard and strong, reaching around from behind.

"Hey, you spilled out," he said, his low voice so gravelly with lust, I could just hear it over my music. But I was distracted with how his hands cupped my breasts, palms beneath the two mounds, fingers over my nipples.

I pulled the headphones off my ears, jaw fallen in surprised shock. But now I could hear him clearly and he leaned over my shoulder, speaking down into my ear with that delicious husk.

"Don't want anyone to see these beauties," he said, but we both knew nobody was gonna see me topless. It was a private section of the beach, and the staff were all from away and barely spoke English, so who cared if they got a peek?

But all that aside, there was still the feeling of my daddy's thick, hard cock brushing against my ass.

It was so delicious. I felt like I'd faint, right then and there. I couldn't believe how intense the sensation of a man touching my breasts could be.

Yea, you got me. Even though I spend most my time reading erotica or watching porn, I've never had a boyfriend, and I've never had *anyone* touch me. Not even my tits. I thought I was going to burst, and my thong bikini bottoms were drenched as I shivered despite the heat.

His large hands held me, lightly stroking my skin, teasing the ever-so-sensitive nipples that peaked those mounds. And his cock, that mighty, veiny shaft, pulsed with life against me.

"Guess I should've bought you a bigger bikini somewhere along the way," he husked into my ear, his voice dripping with sex, so rough and low. "But I just loved how this one fit you so sexily," he admitted, and he nuzzled against my ear and neck.

It was so wrong, but it felt so right. I was breathing heavy, almost unable to speak with how turned on I was. I couldn't believe it was happening, really. I'd dreamed about it for so long, I had to wonder if I had just dozed off in the warm, summer heat.

But he felt too real for it to be a dream.

Besides, if it was a dream, I never, ever wanted to wake up again.

"Daddy, we shouldn't..." I halfheartedly protested, but my hips moved of their own accord. I could feel his cock on my ass, and I started grinding into him, wanting to see what he felt like between my two, tight cheeks.

He parted his full lips to reply, but that thick, supple ass of mine rubbing up on his dick stole the words from him. And any idea of withdrawing and ending this contact left his mind as I worked his thick dick between my two ass cheeks.

"I know baby," he husked finally, a low groan escaping his lips. "But we both know we have to... we can't fight it forever," he said, those big hands of his losing all pretense of just covering me, as he fondled my tits, teased my nipples, even lightly tugged at them.

Maybe I should've gotten out of the house the second I graduated high school. Maybe I should've left him to find another woman his own age. Someone who wasn't a smitten, lust-filled, and virginal schoolgirl.

But he was right. We couldn't fight it forever, because try as we might, our attraction was too strong to deny. I could no more leave him than I could walk away right now.

"Someone might see," I whispered, as if that were my biggest worry about him stealing my innocence.

His hips began to return my ass's motions, and we were grinding our bodies together lewdly, shamelessly in the midday tropical sun. That thick shaft bulging, throbbing with need. For me. All for me.

"Then let 'em watch," he finally growled back, kissing my neck. "I checked us in as husband and wife... this is an adult-only resort..." he said, and finally he let one of those hands leave my breasts, sliding down over my taut tummy, those long fingers of his sliding over the tiny triangle of my thong, running along the outline of my slit.

My breath held, and my heart pounded. I felt so exposed, but it felt so... sexy. I'd never felt so desirable in all my life, and his words just spurred me on. But still, I was nervous. I didn't want him to find out I was a virgin. But I also didn't want to have him take me to the bedroom, then wonder why I wasn't... better. Why I couldn't do all the things those girls did in my pornos.

I worried on my lower lip, my eyes fluttered closed as I just tried to enjoy the sensation of his touches. The fact that he was finally, blissfully, falling for me.

We lost all appreciation of time, our two beautiful bodies rocking and grinding together, his hands fondling my breasts, my pussy, making me moan louder with time. Those lips of his working over my neck, making me bend it to the side and bare it all, eager for his touches.

His lips only broke from my smooth, young skin to mutter filthy things into my ear. Filthy, sweet things.

"You're Daddy's little girl. Always have been, always will be," he said, his growling voice edged with such authority, such command. It wasn't up for debate. No, not ever. It sent a shiver down my spine.

I opened my eyes, the bright sun still blasting down upon me, my sunglasses shielding me from the glare enough that I could see there was another couple coming out of the resort and headed towards their pool in the next room over. Only a few sparse shrubs and palm trees blocked our view of each other. I gasped and tried to slap his hand away, but I miscalculated, instead smacking his fingers against my clit and making me almost buckle over in intense pleasure.

So instead of stopping him, I just made an even better show for the next couple, who stopped to grin and watch. In fact, it only emboldened him.

"Every guy wants to fuck you sweetie, but you're all mine," he husked into my ear as I shivered and moaned, and he took his hand off my thong for one heartbreaking moment. But before I could appreciate that he was ending the public show for the voyeurs, he slipped his fingers *inside* my thong instead!

"He's over there, wishing his woman was you instead," he muttered lowly to me as he teased my clit, working my nipples and whole body so masterfully. "But you belong to Daddy," he growled possessively.

I shut my eyes again, focusing on his words, on the sensation of my body getting ready for him. Getting ready for my first time.

Could I really go through with it though? I knew I wanted to. I wanted it more than I'd ever wanted anything else. But I was still scared.

"I'm a virgin," I finally admitted, squirming against his touch and praying he didn't break away. "I've never... I've never even touched a guy. Or been touched."

All of a sudden, his strong arms and their meticulous, experienced motions ceased, his whole body stilled around me. And I worried he might stop, or be disappointed.

But the thick throb of his huge cock told me that wasn't going to happen. He renewed his groping of my nubile young body, fondling and kissing me. His voice so raw and rough.

"Mmm, you are such a perfect little girl," he said with lusty glee. "Saved yourself for Daddy all these years, didn't you? Admit it," he growled in my ear, driving my body closer towards climax with just his hands.

I didn't want to admit it, but he coaxed it out of me with his skillful touches and his breath against my ear.

"Yes," I whispered, barely audible over the sounds of the waves crashing on the beach, and my heart pounding in my chest. "No one else could compare," I whimpered, and he rewarded my confession. His fingers stroked against my clit adeptly, and as I started buckling forward, he held me in place, making me cum all over his hand, my body rendered useless as the couple stared at our illicit show.

Oh, they tried to look like they weren't staring, but they were. Breathlessly reclining in their own section of the resort, peering over beneath sunglasses.

I caught glimpses of that as I shook in the after effects of the first climax he ever gave me. Well, directly. Not counting the ones he gave me through my own fingers or vibrator as I thought of him.

He slipped his hand from my pussy, and then he licked clean a glistening finger before offering one to me.

"Mmm, you taste like heaven," he rumbled, squeezing me in his arms. "And I bet you'll feel even better once you're wrapped around Daddy's cock."

I took his finger in between my lips, letting my tongue whirl around the pad of his fingertip, feeling the ribbed sensation on my tongue. I moaned around it as he talked about his cock, and I gave a little nod, looking over my shoulder to him.

"We should go back to the room," I said softly.

He took hold of my hip and shoulder, twisted me about so I could look straight up at his dashing, wryly smiling face.

"They'll have to wait for next time to watch us," he said with a playful husk before he just bent down and scooped me up in his arms like I was a child again. Those thick arms of his had no trouble lifting me as he carried me up the stairs back towards the suite.

Yet even then, his eyes couldn't help but soak me in, look at the rippling of my breasts with each motion, my face... his eyes full of desire. And love. That undying, fatherly love that made everything else so much more special.

He left the sliding glass doors open as he took me inside, through the main room to the bedroom.

With care, he laid me out on the bed like I really was his bride and this really was our honeymoon. His two large hands, sliding up my legs to my waist, to grasp my thong and tug it down, leaving me naked except for the bikini top which dangled like a necklace.

"You're the most beautiful girl in the world," he said as he shed his own shorts, letting that beast of a cock spring out, thick and long.

It was the first cock I'd ever seen in the flesh. I was fascinated by it. It was so much bigger than I expected, with ribbed veins pulsing each time his heart beat. I reached out, my little fingers wrapping around it, barely able to contain his girth.

I looked up at him, gnawing on my lower lip, wondering what to do next.

"Don't worry," he husked as he climbed up onto the California-King-sized bed. "Leave everything to Daddy," he said, that same phrase he always used to reassure me, like when I fussed about packing for this trip, only to surprise me with a shopping trip once we got here, all new clothes... except my bikini.

His strong hands parted my long legs, spreading me open before him as he tugged his cock from my grasp a moment, and bent down. He kissed my breast, teased my nipple, then showered my skin with more affection down over my tummy, then along my soft inner thighs.

"I just need a taste before I claim this pussy," he rumbled, lashing his tongue over my slit then devouring me with such a hunger.

"Ah!" I screamed, surprised by the intensity of the sensation, feeling so good! It wasn't like with his fingers, or my fingers, or even my vibrator. It was something totally new, and so delicious. I didn't even have time to be nervous about how I tasted, or what I felt like against his tongue, because my hands were already balling into fists as electricity started gathering in my clit and threatening to spread over my entire body.

"I'm gonna... I'm gonna," I gasped out, seconds before my body began to convulse, and my honey soaked his lips and chin.

He kept it up after that, my squeals and cries only urging him on, torturing me with overpowering pleasure until I was pushing at his broad shoulders, begging him, "Please Daddy! Stop!"

He rose up from my pussy, a grin on his face as he licked his lips, wiped away the glistening excess of honey from his jaw to savor that too. And his shaft was still so iron hard as he rose up over me, giving me such a perfect view of that hard, muscular body.

"That's the only pussy I ever want to eat again," he rumbled as he took hold of my legs in his hands then dove down, kissing my lips with a passionate desire as his cock came down to rest heavily against my mound with a smack.

I wasn't on birth control, and he knew it, we talked about that stuff openly after all. But he didn't reach for a condom either. Not that I assumed he had any on him. He surely hadn't been planning on stealing my innocence on a spur of the moment.

I didn't have any time to wonder if what we were doing was right or not. I knew the risks, and I was so scared, but... I kind of liked it too.

What would I do if he took my virginity, then got me pregnant? Sure, I'd heard the rumors you couldn't get pregnant your first time, but I'd been on the internet. I knew you absolutely could.

I wondered if that was something on his mind. Or if he was just so caught up in the moment he wasn't thinking straight... I had no way of knowing, and before I could ask, I felt his swollen crown rub along my slick little slit, and it was the best thing I'd ever felt in my life.

Then I felt him start pressing into my virginal pussy, pushing past that little remaining sliver of resistance.

He stretched out my hymen as he edged his thick cock inside me, and we both watched it all. Our eyes sweeping down over our two stunning bodies, locked on where they met. Neither of us wanted to miss a moment of this, we wanted to burn it into our minds forever: that moment where my daddy took my virginity, and made me officially a woman.

He grunted, his dick throbbed, and I felt a pang of pain, but he rocked his hips and eased his dick into me. There was no way to make it completely painless, not with how damn big that shaft of his was. Thankfully the pleasure of our raw loins rubbing together made up for everything else.

"Ohhh baby," he groaned, finally arching his head back as he sank in halfway, feeling my tight little pussy stretched around his shaft, clenching his girth. "Fuck, you have the best pussy I've ever felt," he rumbled, pumping his hips, going a little deeper with each new motion.

I was so wet, even my inner thighs were soaked with my juices, and I wrapped my legs around him. My arms clung to his neck, wanting to hold him tight, even though I also wanted to watch him impale me. It was such a confusing mess of emotions, but all of them were... amazing. To say the least.

Every night before that night, every time I ever tried to get myself off, any experimenting I'd done paled in comparison to how the real thing felt. It was taboo, it was so wrong, but maybe that's one of the reasons it felt so good.

"Ah," I whimpered into his ear, trying to hold on and not cum immediately as he finally hit my deepest point. "Ah... you'll pull out, right?"

His powerful body shifted above me, muscles rippling as he pulled back, and then began to thrust into me at a rising pace. He grunted, his dick throbbed, and he bit my neck, then my ear, all before he ever got to answer me.

"I'd never dream of pulling out of this perfect little pussy and ruining your first time," he growled, holding himself up on just one hand as he used the other to tug away my bikini top entirely, toss it to the floor and grope my heavy breasts.

"You're Daddy's girl now," he said loud amid his pants and moans. "You have to take Daddy bareback, sweetie."

That was the straw that broke the camel's back and made me cum for the very first time on his cock. It was so embarrassing, letting him know in such a loud way that his words... They sent me careening over the edge of civility.

My pussy clenched his cock, my fists filled with blankets as I spasmed beneath him. I was so sensitive after already getting off so many times, but he wasn't giving me any rest. He was making me take his thick, raw cock, and not letting me shy away from the intense pleasure at all.

I caught glimpses of him, heard his voice, and knew I nearly made him bust then too. But he held on, by force of will and practiced experience against the tight clinging of my virginal pussy, wanting to savor our first time a little longer.

He grew harder, his heavy balls slapping against my bubbly ass as he picked up his pace. He rumbled, roared, his pace growing erratic.

"I'm gonna cum baby... beg for it. Beg for me to knock your pretty little pussy up," he commanded me, like he was laying down the law about homework and not his intent to knock his own little girl up.

I could barely breathe. I was so swept up in the moment, and my head rolled back, our bodies interlaced together. I was determined to bring him over the edge. To not shy away from his need to cum in me. I wanted it. I wanted him. So I did what the girls in my pornos do.

"Ahh, Daddy! I want you to fucking cum in me! I want you to breed me," I begged, my face flushing at just how dirty I sounded.

He loved it. His dick swelled, he let loose a deep roar. He squeezed my hip and breast as he arched his spine and then buried his dick inside me.

"Miiine!" he roared just a split second before he came. That thick cock spasming, blowing long, creamy jets of his virile seed deep inside my unprotected pussy, blasting it right against my womb as the bed quaked beneath us.

But in the afterglow of our fucking, his fingers found my hair, and he looked at me with such love and affection. And that didn't feel dirty, not at all. Even though his dick was still lodged within me, and I lost count of how many times he'd made me cum, it all felt very romantic.

Like we really were just two people, newly married and deeply in love with each other. I knew then, at that very moment, that I would never regret what we did. And his mouth found mine, and by the end of the night, we'd made love twice more.

It was only tempting fate that I would get knocked up, and sure enough, two months later, I broke him the news. And his smile... Well, I wish I'd gotten a picture of it. I'd never seen him so happy in all my life.

But what really shocked me was what he did next.

He got down on his knee, took a ring out of his pants pocket, and proposed right then and there. Of course, we had to rush the wedding so I'd still fit into my dress walking down the aisle...

And now, here I am. At home, as spring finally sends a warmth into the air and new life is breathed into the world, rubbing my swollen stomach and wondering when you'll come. Not that I'll ever tell my little girl the story of how she came into the world.

That's a secret for daddies and mommies.

THE END
Get Access to over 20 more FREE Erotica Downloads at Shameless Book Deals

SHAMELESS BOOK DEALS is a website that shamelessly brings you the very best erotica at the best prices from the best authors to your inbox every day. Sign up to our newsletter to get access to the daily deals and the Shameless Free Story Archive!

SHAMELESS BOOK DEALS

The best place to get erotica recommendations tailored to you! Sign up for the newsletter below and find out why it's so good to be shameless! Free stories for subscribers.

Newsletter Sign Up

MORE FROM SHAMELESS BOOK PRESS

Anything for the Man of the House (Ten Brats Who Learn How to Behave): These brats can pout all they want, they are going to do anything for the man of the house, even if what he demands is to take them hard and most certainly without using protection or pulling out. These stories are totally taboo and will leave you panting!

Submit to the Man of the House (Ten Brats who Give him Anything he Wants): The **brats** in these stories are about to give up their most carefully guarded treasures for flaunting those perfect little **fertile** bodies in front of the **men of their houses**. When these men decide that it's time for the little princesses to give them an **heir**, it's going to happen just the way they like it. **Hard, unprotected and all night long** even if it is the brat's **first time**.

Satisfy the Man of the House (Ten Brats who Give him Anything he Wants): These brats can pout all they want, they are going to satisfy the man of the house, even if what he demands is to take them hard and most certainly without using protection or pulling out. These stories are totally taboo and will leave you panting!

Taken 54 Times (54 Men. 10 Women. You Do The Math):
How many could you handle? Two? Three? A dozen muscular athletes? How about trying all fifty-four? The women in these ten stories are taken hard every which way and just when they think it's over, there's another man who is just beginning. They are left messy, panting and oh so satisfied!

Owned by the Man of the House (Ten Brats who Learn how to Please Him): The man of the house lays claim to everything *in* his house, and that includes these precious little brats who think that they can get away with flaunting their perfect fertile bodies in front of him. When he decides to take what is his, he's going to take his pleasure **hard, unprotected and all night long**. They'll find how difficult it is to maintain a princess-pout when they're screaming his name.

Shameless Submission (Ten Perfect Princesses Bend to his Will): True Masters come from all walks of life, some of them are the very pillars of our society, some of them are in our own homes. What they all have in common is that when they choose you as their submissive, you're left writhing in ecstasy, bent to their will, and life will never be the same again.

Ravished by the Man of the House (Ten Brats who Learn How to Please Him): Those perfect pouts have been getting these little princesses everything they wanted for years. Now, for the first time, all they're getting is into the best kind of trouble with the Man of the House. They are going to be left a sweaty mess, legs quivering too hard to stand, and full of his special gift.

Printed in the USA
CPSIA information can be obtained
at www.ICGtesting.com
LVHW052311290823
756688LV00020BA/286